THE PEPPERMINT TREE

KRISTY MCCAFFREY

The Peppermint Tree

Cover Design: Earthly Charms – earthlycharms.com

Editor: Mimi The Grammar Chick – merrelli.wixsite.com/grammarchick

Proofreader: Diane Garland – yourworldkeeper.com/

Author Photo: Katy McCaffrey – instagram.com/katymccaffreyphoto

E-book ISBN-13: 978-1-7331420-6-9

Print ISBN-13: 978-1-7331420-7-6

kristymccaffrey.com

kristy@kristymccaffrey.com

❀ Created with Vellum

Chapter One

---

*S*outhwestern Colorado
December

SKYE MALLORY SQUINTED through her windshield as the wiper blades danced back and forth. The weather on this dark December night had turned awful with heavy snowflakes consuming the sky as if the heavens had released a deluge of white feathers. Before she'd left Denver and the haven of her condo, she had checked the forecast, and in her mind had decided it was navigable. But life hadn't been going her way of late and this was no exception. No reason to be surprised that this had turned into a bit more than she'd bargained for.

She slowed her Prius. It wasn't great in the snow, but as she now spent most of her time within city limits that included well-maintained winter roads, it hadn't really been a problem. Usually she had more time to plan before driving south to visit her family and The Quarter-Circle, a sprawling five-thousand acre cattle ranch.

But then Mrs. Pendleton had died, naming Skye her sole heir. Skye had never been more stunned than when the will had arrived in the mail, stating that she now owned five hundred acres and the Pendleton Ranch.

Correction. It was a close second to the shock of Joe Carrigan telling her no in high school.

Why did that rejection still sting like it had happened yesterday?

She released a disgusted grunt, since she was alone in her car.

It had been nine years of silence from the one who'd gotten away.

He didn't get away. He never wanted me in the first place.

She tried to avoid thinking about the fact that Joe Carrigan had returned to the area six months ago. Her mother had informed her one afternoon via a phone call, gushing that it was so great to have Joey and his mom back after the unfortunate death of his dad. Skye had been sorry to hear that Buck Carrigan had passed, because she'd always liked him. But the news had made her less than thrilled to come home for a visit. Joe Carrigan had purchased the Triple C Ranch, which coincidentally bordered not only on Mallory's land but none other than the Pendleton Ranch.

Did the guy upstairs have it out for her?

In the last six months, she'd had a botched tooth extraction requiring endless visits to the dentist, her stock investments had dropped by half, and douche-bag Dave, a fellow attorney she was dating, had stolen her firm's biggest client right out from under her.

She muttered a few swear words simply because it made her feel better. Dave hadn't been a love connection by any stretch, but she'd been proud of herself for trying to be less work and more play, and all it had gotten her in the end was a place on her boss's naughty list. She seriously doubted she'd be receiving a Christmas bonus after that debacle.

And then she'd gotten word of Mrs. Pendleton's passing, filling her with a heavy grief, while also stunning her with the woman's puzzling generosity. While Skye had spent a lot of time with the widow back in high school, she hadn't seen her in over two years. What could it mean? Because some tiny part of her flared to life at the prospect of returning to the Durango area. To her home. To Joe.

Why in God's name was he there? Why couldn't he just have stayed away?

If she decided to set up house on the Pendleton property, she would be his neighbor. Despite several hundred acres separating the actual dwellings, it would still be too close for her.

She grumbled aloud again.

Stop thinking.

It had always been her problem. She was an analyzer. She picked things apart. It was why she was a good lawyer. Well, except for the recent client loss. She sighed. Maybe she should accept that broker's offer to freelance for his land company.

First things first—she had a Monday morning meeting in Durango with Mrs. Pendleton's attorney, Brian Fogle. She needed to learn the particulars of her inheritance.

Skye regretted that she hadn't been able to get away from work for the funeral three days ago; she was determined to at least make the attorney meeting.

And honestly, aside from this nerve-wracking storm, she had been glad for the excuse to come home for the holidays early. It was two weeks until Christmas, but rather than rush back to Denver after the Pendleton business was taken care of, she planned to stay and sleep in her childhood bed, drink hot chocolate under a cozy blanket, and watch Christmas movies while her mom made pot roast or lasagna, or some other delectable treat that reminded Skye of simpler times. With her holiday shopping complete, she could kick back and pretend she was twelve again instead of a weathered and battered twenty-six.

Visibility was bad, her headlights shining into a white background that revealed little else. She was barely able to stay on the road by following the guideposts that were still peeking out of several inches of snow on the ground.

Skye gripped the steering wheel, a wave of anxiety pushing through her.

Maybe she should turn around and return to Durango, but the thought of making a U-turn in this made her nerves dance. She could simply stop, but someone might rear-end her. And there really was no place to pull over.

However, she was getting close to Hank's Bar. A mile or two, maybe? She could stop there, hunker down with a glass of white wine, and wait out the storm. She had called her parents earlier in the day to tell them she was coming, but they hadn't picked up, so she'd left a message on their archaic answering machine.

As if on cue, her phone buzzed. She grabbed it from the console where she'd stashed it.

"Hello?"

"Skylar?" It was her father. "Are you driving, honey?"

"Yeah. I'm between Durango and Hesperus. But it's really coming down."

"Be careful. Can you pull off somewhere? I'm going to call Oliver to come get you."

Skye's back ached from leaning forward. "I'm almost to Hank's. Tell Ollie to meet me there."

"Okay. Call me when you arrive."

Skye chanced a glance down to end the call, then looked up as she fumbled to put the phone back in the console. Suddenly her tires turned and with only one hand on the wheel the car veered to the right. She jerked the steering to the left but overcompensated, and the vehicle fish-tailed, sliding off the road and sinking into a trough before coming to a stop.

JOE CARRIGAN WATCHED as the red taillights in the distance slid from left to right and then right even more, finally stopping. He'd been following the Prius for a while, and the driver had been conservative, but their luck had just run out. He was in his Bronco—the same one he'd driven in high school on these very roads—and it could still be trusted in bad weather. He'd been able to afford better cars over the years, but he still had a habit of jumping in this one, especially on a night like this.

He checked his rearview mirror. Thankfully, no cars behind him. He slowed the Bronco and guided it as far to the right as he could without getting stuck.

Stepping out of his vehicle, a blast of cold air hit him as heavy snowflakes engulfed him. He really shouldn't be out in this, but he'd agreed to meet Oliver and Celeste and a friend of Celeste's, a blind date he'd been badgered into. His life had been too busy of late for a woman, but it didn't mean he actually needed or wanted one in his life.

He reached inside the Bronco and grabbed his heavy canvas coat, quickly pulling it on and zipping it to his neck. The snow crunched beneath his boots and his breath came out in white puffs as he crossed the beam of his headlights and approached the Prius. He tapped on the driver's window, the shadowy figure of a woman on the other side. She hesitated a moment then rolled the window down.

"Are you all right, miss?"

As the woman's face became fully visible, he did a double-take. "Skylar?"

Her forehead pinched into hard ridges, and her eyes registered a flash of outrage. "Carrigan?"

As if a freight train had hit him, he uttered, "It's been a long time."

"You don't say. What are you doing here?"

Corralling his thoughts, he said, "I moved back six months ago. I bought the Three C Ranch."

"I know." Her face shifted into a slightly less offensive glare, her skin blanching white in the process. "I heard. I mean, what are you doing out in *this*?"

Over the years, he had wondered what it would be like to see her again, but now that the moment was here, he wasn't prepared for it. In high school, she had been quiet and wickedly smart, both a determined tomboy and a girly-girl, a combination that was uniquely Skye. She had always caught his eye—once they'd hit high school, it had been difficult to ignore her curves—but for his own self-preservation, he'd stayed away from her, in the romantic sense at least, even when she had made a play for him, a memory he rarely revisited.

But the woman facing him now—the playful lips, the creamy complexion offset by dark auburn hair, and the expressive eyes that had always intimidated him—reignited the fire that had smoldered for years.

"I'm on my way to meet your brother and Celeste down at Hank's. I thought you lived in Denver." He'd learned in the past few months that she was a lawyer. No husband. No children.

"I do." She frowned. "Ollie and Celeste?"

"You didn't know about them?" He didn't think it was a secret that Oliver Mallory had developed a hunger for Celeste Bailey, but if Skye didn't know about her brother and her lifelong best friend, then maybe Ollie didn't want it advertised just yet.

"I don't think it's serious," he added, but he knew that was a lie. "Are you headed to Hank's?"

"Yeah," she replied, "I'm supposed to meet Ollie for a ride, or at least that's what my dad said when I talked to him a few minutes ago. But I didn't know Ollie was on a date with Celeste, and I'm guessing my dad didn't know either."

The snowfall had stopped, but it would likely begin again. He opened her car door. "C'mon, I'll drive you to Hank's. You shouldn't stay here. Someone might hit you."

"You don't have to," she said. "I can call Ollie to come get me here."

"Still stubborn. I'm not leaving you stranded by the side of the road, Skye." He motioned for her to exit the vehicle. "Besides, it'll give us a chance to catch up."

For a brief moment, she reminded him of a cornered possum, her eyes darting around for an escape route. But she gave a nod, put her car into park, and turned off the ignition. She collected keys, purse, and a coat then tried to leave the Prius, but it was angled in the snow bank, and she fell back into her seat. Leaning down, he grabbed her hand and yanked her out, bringing her close enough that he caught a whiff of her flowery scent and loose strands of her hair caressed his cheek.

She immediately put distance between them. Her blue eyes, visible now in the headlights, locked with his. Clad in a snug ivory sweater and jeans, she had grown from bewitching girl to gorgeous woman without missing a beat.

Opening the door to the backseat, she struggled to pull

out a suitcase, the messy bun at the nape of her neck bouncing up and down.

"Here, let me help." He ushered her aside.

"Okay," she said, her voice breathless and strained.

"You planning to stay for a while?" he asked as he retrieved two suitcases.

"Hopefully through the New Year."

He grabbed one more bag and a briefcase, which she reached for, careful to avoid touching his hand.

"I'm not contagious," he teased.

"What?"

They locked eyes again.

"You seem stressed," he said. "You didn't hurt yourself when you hit the snow bank, did you?"

"No." She repositioned her coat over her arm and tugged the straps of her purse back onto her shoulder. "I'm fine. A little rattled, that's all." She gifted with him with the fakest smile he'd ever seen.

There had been a time when he and Skye had been buddies, the only female friend he'd ever had. He couldn't blame her, he supposed, for feeling awkward around him— he'd left town without saying goodbye nine years ago and had never bothered to stay in touch. It had seemed easier that way.

He turned and headed to his Bronco.

"You still have this thing?" she said.

"It's stood the test of time." He secured her bags in the back and came to open her car door, but she'd already settled herself into the passenger's seat. He got behind the wheel and started inching the vehicle forward once again on the snow-covered road.

As Skye pushed strands of hair away from her face, Joe kept his gaze forward to avoid staring. He wondered if she still had the handful of freckles on her nose and cheeks. It had always been his favorite feature of hers. Growing up, she'd been a country girl through and through, but she had always possessed a certain sophistication that had somehow been innate. She had been the girl he admired, the girl who had always disarmed him with her intellect, and when she was older, the girl he had been careful to keep at arm's length.

Then his dad had announced he was selling the Carrigan Ranch and uprooting Joe and his mom north to Estes Park.

A clean break had always worked best for Joe, and he'd seen no reason to change that method, so he had put Skye Mallory into a place in his thoughts where desire and longing couldn't bother him. He'd always been good at that.

Striving to keep his tone neutral, he asked, "How have you been?"

"Busy. You?"

"Can't complain."

"I heard about your dad. I'm sorry."

"Thanks." Buck Carrigan had died in January, and Joe was still sucker-punched by it. As ornery as his old man had been, he'd always had a soft spot for Skye.

"You were one of his favorites," he said, sneaking a glance at her.

She rewarded him with a hint of a smile. "He was one of mine. But he sure could be scary when he wanted. Remember the time you, me, and Ollie took the tractor out, and it got stuck in that ravine, and your dad had to get a bunch of the neighbors with their trucks to pull it out? When he lectured us about how disappointed he was, I wanted to curl into a ball and disappear."

Joe laughed. "Yeah, he was mad, but later he told that story with a smile plastered all over his face. He referred to the three of us as The Good, The Bad, and The Ugly."

"Who was The Ugly?" she demanded.

"Ollie, but don't tell him."

"That seems about right," she said with a hint of satisfaction.

Joe turned the Bronco into Hank's, several cars covered in varying layers of snow dotting the parking lot. The weather hadn't been enough to keep the crowds away. It was Friday night, after all. He made his own makeshift parking spot and shut off the car.

"So which one of us was The Good?" she asked.

He turned to look at her. "You, of course."

She hadn't donned her coat and the rapid rise and fall of her chest became noticeable as her breathing increased. In the harsh glow of the parking lot light, her cheeks took on a rosy flush that sent his thoughts to one place—kissing her.

"That would make you The Bad." Her quiet voice broke through the stillness in the darkened cab. She abruptly released her seatbelt from the buckle and clutched her large purse to her chest. "Well, thanks for the ride. I'll wait inside until Ollie arrives." She grabbed the door handle for a hasty exit.

"I'll buy you a beer," he said.

She swung her gaze back to him, her eyes wide.

"I'm meeting Ollie and Celeste, remember?" he added. *Along with a woman Celeste was supposedly bringing along.* For one wild moment, he wondered if the blind date was Skye, causing a surge of anticipation to slice through him. But she wasn't. Celeste had said he didn't know the woman, but she was sure he would hit it off with her. The chance of that had seemed slim to none at the time he had agreed, and now with a thudding certainty, it was none.

Seeing Skye had sealed that deal.

Skye nodded stiffly, then slipped out of the Bronco into the blustery winter wonderland.

Joe exited the vehicle and trailed behind her to the

entrance. He moved past her to open the large wooden door of Hank's, and she bumped into him, meeting his eyes briefly before she moved quickly inside.

He had been dragging his feet about coming tonight but now was glad that he'd ventured out. The blind date hadn't been his fate after all. It had been finding Skye Mallory on the side of the road.

Chapter Two

*S*kye entered Hank's, stepping from the mud room into the main restaurant with Joe Carrigan following her. "Rock the Casbah" blared on the speakers, putting her right back in high school.

With her stomach in knots and her hands trembling, she could only wonder at the cosmic joke of Carrigan finding her as soon as she hit town. She had figured she'd be able to avoid him for months—maybe even years—before bumping into him at, say, the grocery store. At least in that instance, she could've hidden in the next aisle and slinked out before he ever saw her.

A hostess appeared. "You guys are brave to be out in this."

"Are you open?" Skye asked, trying to ignore the tall, dark, and handsome guy standing beside her.

"Yep. You want a table or just want to sit at the bar?"

"How about a table?" Joe cut in. "We have more joining us."

As the girl led them to the far side of the establishment, Skye noticed that Hank's still had the same rustic interior and sawdust-covered floor. Joe grabbed a table with six chairs. Were they expecting more than Ollie and Celeste? How in the world had she not known that her brother and her best friend were seeing each other? She could understand why Ollie might not tell her—it wasn't like the two of them chatted intimately about their love lives—but Celeste? Her oldest and closest girlfriend?

The hurt was kept at bay for only one reason, and he was currently pulling out her chair.

She hung the coat she hadn't bothered to wear on a hook on the wall—seeing Carrigan had cranked up her internal temperature—then sat, trying her best to ignore him as she tucked her purse beside her. He rounded the opposite side of the table, shed his heavy jacket, and sat directly across from her.

She surreptitiously noted that he hadn't changed much in the looks department: his physique was still lean and coiled beneath the grey thermal pullover he wore; his brown eyes still reflected little emotion, a fact that had been driven home on that day so long ago when he'd rejected her. Despite having had several boyfriends in the ensuing years, both serious and casual, no man had ever come close to Carrigan.

Sarcasm echoed in her head. *What a lovely end to an already awful day.*

She needed a drink.

"Can I get you both waters?" the hostess asked, handing each of them a menu.

"I'll have a Whiskey Sour," Skye said. If she was going to be forced to make small talk with Carrigan after a nine-year absence from her life, she needed fortification. Besides, Ollie would drive her to their parents' ranch, so if she was a bit tipsy, no problem.

"I'll have whatever's on tap," Carrigan said.

Although Skye wasn't hungry, she opened the menu and

began perusing it in earnest. "Thank you for stopping to help me," she murmured without looking up.

"I'd been following you for a while. I had no idea it was you."

So his heroic actions weren't really for *her*, but a general thing. Goddamned kismet and goddamned fate. She should've hunkered down in Durango, but she'd convinced herself that she could make it to The Quarter-Circle.

Her stomach knotted tighter.

The waitress appeared with their drinks, and Skye took hold of hers, wanting to appease her anxiety as soon as possible.

"How about a toast?" he asked, forcing her to halt the liquor mid-air.

A toast wasn't really on her mind, but she raised her glass a smidge. Wouldn't want to be rude and all that.

"It's good to see you again, Skye." He clinked his pilsner against hers.

She gave a half-hearted smile and a nod, then took a big gulp of fortification.

Why had she always had it so bad for Joe Carrigan?

She only knew the basics of his return, since she had made a point *not* to ask about him when speaking with her parents or Oliver in the past few months. With her Christmas spirit slipping away, she steeled herself. It was time to get it over with and hear all about his beautiful wife, three gorgeous children who all resembled him, and his extraordinary life in general. She took another drink of courage. "What have you been up to the last nine years?"

"Well, if you're wondering if all that tutoring you gave me in high school worked, it did. For a little while, at least. I went to UC Boulder for a few semesters, but I didn't finish."

"Why not?"

He gave a slight shrug and leaned back in his chair. Her

gaze flicked to the beer glass he fingered with a hand that worked the land and not a computer.

"My dad wanted me at the ranch, and truthfully, I wanted to go back. I came to realize that classrooms and books weren't my thing."

"I heard the ranch in Estes Park was quite impressive."

He nodded. "It was."

"But you sold it? To come back here?"

He took a drink of his beer, and then remained quiet for a moment. "Estes Park was my dad's dream. And he worked hard at it. Maybe too hard. One day, he had a heart attack in the kitchen. And he was gone, just like that."

"I'm sorry." And she meant it. "There was no one quite like your dad."

His gaze softened, and he seemed to share her sentiment. "I know." He raked a hand through his black hair. "My mom was having a tough time, and the ranch was a lot of work. I suggested we downsize, and I realized that she was interested in returning here. The old Carrigan Ranch wasn't available, but the Three C was."

"Skye?" Her brother's booming voice drew her attention from Carrigan.

Oliver strode up to the table, dressed in a white button-down shirt and nicer jeans than he normally wore. While he'd gone to college in Arizona, in the end he'd returned to a rancher's life much like Carrigan had. He ran his own small spread to the southwest while remaining involved in The Quarter-Circle with her mom and dad.

Skye stood to hug her brother. His hair, more burnished than hers, was looking presentable for once. He smelled good, too. He was definitely on a date. And that girl was right behind him.

"Skylar!" Celeste, her long blond hair flowing down her

shoulders, grinned broadly as she scooped Skye into an embrace. "Why didn't you tell me you were coming?"

"It was last minute."

Another woman lingered behind them. Celeste ushered her forward. "This is Tina."

The petite, brown-haired woman shook Skye's hand and then Joe's. As everyone moved to sit down, Skye noticed that Celeste made sure Tina was beside Carrigan.

Celeste took a spot next to Skye, and Ollie took residence at the end.

"Why didn't you call?" Ollie asked her.

"Dad said he was going to get a hold of you to meet me here," Skye said, not really wanting to admit that she'd lost control of her car. "Did you talk to him?"

"No." Ollie pulled out his cellphone. "I missed a call from him, though. How'd you two find each other?" he asked, looking from her to Joe.

The waitress appeared and took drink orders for the three new arrivals.

"I saw her in the parking lot," Carrigan said, his tone flat. That he was covering for the fact that she'd slid off the road—and throwing Ollie off the scent of harassing her for bad driving—was enough to make her heart flutter. But then he did something that caught her completely off guard—he held her gaze with a flirty twinkle in his eye.

Alarm bells went off in her head. Scratch that. It was more like a blazing siren.

In high school, no matter how much she'd wanted him to look at her the way he had Sheila Walters or Bella Brookstone, he never had. Not once. It had been up to her to make the first move, and the result was a swift crash and burn of the two-year bubble that Skye had built in her head filled with nothing but the two of them.

Certain that she had misread the situation, she diverted

her attention, because if her intuition was right, then Tina was here for only one reason. This was a double date. And Skye was the infamous fifth wheel.

"You all were planning a get together tonight?" Skye said to Celeste. "In this weather?"

Celeste laughed, and Skye didn't miss the nervous under-current. "Yeah, we just wanted to grab a beer. And Tina is new in town. She works with me at the print shop. I wanted to get her out to meet more people."

"Where are you from?" Skye asked the woman, deter-mined to ignore Carrigan.

"Dallas," she replied.

"That's a change of scenery. How do you like it here?"

"It's great," Tina replied, moving her napkin aside so the waitress could set a frosty glass of amber beer in front of her. "But I'm looking forward to spring."

Everyone laughed.

Celeste took a drink of her frothy ale and said to Skye, "I didn't think you were coming until Christmas Eve." She added for Tina's benefit, "Skye lives in Denver." To which Tina gave a polite nod.

"I decided to take some vacation days," Skye said, reaching for the bowl of peanuts that Celeste had somehow commandeered, not wanting to mention the inheritance yet, at least not until she had a handle on exactly *what* she had inherited. Maybe Mrs. Pendleton's house was falling apart and overrun with mice. Maybe the land was fallow. Maybe the old lady was haunting the place. That caused her to smile. She added, "Things at work have been complicated. I'll tell you about it later."

Skye made the mistake of glancing at Carrigan. His hooded gaze bore into her, and she almost turned to look behind her for the woman that he was obviously shooting lusty thoughts toward, because it sure as hell wasn't her.

On top of everything else, she now had to contend with broken radar when it came to men.

Man, she needed another drink.

"You can come to the Ball tomorrow," Celeste said.

The Mistletoe Ball was an event her folks and many of the people in Durango and the surrounding communities attended every Christmas, and Skye had forgotten completely about it. The last one she'd attended had been five years ago.

Celeste glanced around the table. "We're all going. I even got a ticket for Tina."

Carrigan's date.

An invisible anvil clobbered Skye's chest. He hadn't professed to having a wife and kids, so obviously Celeste was playing matchmaker. She had done it plenty over the years, meddling regularly in Skye's own love life. It was the exact reason Skye had never confided in her best friend about Carrigan. She hadn't wanted Celeste plotting and planning, no matter her good intentions.

But now Skye would have a front-row seat to the Carrigan and Tina show.

"I don't have a dress," she said quickly. "But thanks anyway."

She avoided looking at Carrigan by draining the rest of her Whiskey Sour.

"Did you know about Mrs. Pendleton?" Celeste asked, oblivious to Skye's taut nerves. "She passed away in a nursing home in Cortez a few days ago."

"Yeah, I heard," Skye said. "I was sorry to hear it. She was a nice lady."

Ollie waved over the waitress for another round of drinks. "But a thorn in Joe's side," he said.

Skye glanced at Joe. "How so?"

He gave a slight shake of his head. "I'll tell you about it sometime. It's not that important."

"Remember The Peppermint Tree?" Celeste asked.

"What's that?" Tina asked.

Celeste leaned forward. "It's this odd-shaped tree that sits on the corner of Mrs. Pendleton's property."

"It's a pine tree that's bowed at the top," Oliver added, "so it kind of looks like a candy cane."

"It's always been a spot where the kids congregated," Celeste continued. "Luckily, Mrs. Pendleton never got mad about any of us trespassing. She would even decorate it every Christmas with big ornaments. You could see it from the highway."

"My mom met my dad at the tree," Joe said.

That was news to Skye, but before she could say anything, Tina turned to him and said, "That's really romantic. Celeste told me that your dad recently died. My mom passed last year, so I know how hard it can be."

Skye was forced to watch while Joe and Tina bonded over the death of a parent, feeling even lower for resenting their shared connection. She would be devastated if she lost either of her folks, and she should respect that maybe talking about it would make the other feel a tiny bit better.

She should leave.

A glance at her brother, however, made it clear that it wouldn't be happening anytime soon. He was here with Celeste, and Tina was meant for Carrigan. And Carrigan must have known, since he'd grabbed a table that could seat five instead of four.

She finished off a second, then a third, and finally a fourth Whiskey Sour in the hope of killing off any feelings for Carrigan that dared to show themselves in her heart. She'd been so sure that she was over him, but her discomfort from watching pert, cute Tina befriend him told her that nine years had done nothing to give her perspective on the damned man.

To further drown her sorrows, she stuffed down a hamburger and fries. She reasoned that she needed the food to absorb the alcohol in her stomach.

"You still eat like a lumberjack," Carrigan said.

Gee, thanks.

"Ollie, we should leave," she said, her need to end this evening reaching a flashpoint. "Mom and Dad will be worried."

"You're just gonna leave your car at Hank's?" her brother asked.

Nuts. Time to confess her predicament, but Carrigan cut her off.

"I'll take you back to your folks, Skye," he said.

"No," Celeste cut in. "We'll take her." Then she said to Joe, "Maybe you can take Tina home?"

"If it's all the same, I'll run Skye home," Joe replied coolly. "It's on my way."

Was it? Skye tried to remember the location of the Triple C. Didn't it border The Quarter-Circle? Despite squeezing her brain into thought, she couldn't remember.

She decided to keep her mouth shut. Her bags were already in Carrigan's Bronco anyway, and this way she wouldn't have to admit to Oliver that her car was stuck in a snow bank somewhere.

"Could you give Tina a ride?" Celeste asked Joe. "Ollie and I have to help my dad with something."

Lame, Celeste.

"She's just a few miles back toward Durango," Celeste added, smiling. "It's not far."

Then drive her home yourself! Skye was satisfied that she was only behaving like a B in her head. Right? She looked at everyone closely to see if they'd reacted to her outburst, but they all continued to ignore her and speak only with each other. Somehow, Carrigan agreed to Celeste's suggestion, and Skye frowned.

Super. Now it was a threesome.

While Joe pulled out his wallet and threw several bills onto the table, Skye stood and collected her coat, making a conscious effort to keep herself from swaying.

Maybe I drank a bit too much.

Once bundled up, they all herded out of Hank's. Somehow, Carrigan ended up behind her, and even through her coat she could feel his hand on her lower back.

What the hell? Quit acting like you like me, Carrigan.

She almost said it aloud. She wasn't sure how much more time with Joe Carrigan she could handle before she rounded on him like an angry bear.

Carrigan might still entertain the idea that they could once again be friends like they'd been for most of their childhood, but Skye knew deep in her bones that she couldn't handle it. And it depressed her more than she ever would have thought possible.

It had been nine years, but it were as if no time at all had passed since he'd left her heart in pieces.

Chapter Three

*A*s Carrigan departed Hank's, "Kiss You All Over" played in the background, and the irony didn't escape him. This had been one of his haunts in high school, and he'd romanced many a girl on these very premises. Except the only one that had mattered, the one walking ahead of him like he was escorting her to the gallows. As Skye had sat across the table from him, her pretty face had alternated between fear and obstinance. All directed at him.

Maybe he should just kiss her, to set the record straight between them, because one thing was certain. He was far more interested in Skylar Mallory than Tina ... he couldn't even remember her last name. He was sorry he'd ever agreed to meet Celeste and Ollie tonight for this blind date disguised as a casual get-together, except that it had brought Skye back into his life.

Heavy snowflakes rained down as he led the women to his Bronco. When he opened the passenger door, Tina was at his elbow, so he reluctantly let her climb in first, putting her between him and Skye on the bench seat.

When life hands you lemons, throw them back.

His dad's voice echoed in his head.

He climbed into the driver's seat and left Hank's parking lot, turning on the wipers to help with visibility against the swirling dance of snow glowing in his headlights, and headed down the white-covered highway at a grandma's pace, although there was evidence that a snowplow had recently made a sweep of the road.

"I can't believe this weather," Tina said.

"It's not a great night to be out," Joe replied.

Anchoring her elbow against the door, Skye propped her head up with her hand and yawned.

He glanced around Tina. "Don't pass out on me yet, Mallory."

"Yes, sir," she mumbled, but her eyes drifted shut.

Tina's place was in the opposite direction of The Quarter-Circle, and he'd headed toward Tina's as soon as he left Hank's. He would drop her off first. He could avoid being alone with her, and with Skye mostly passed out, she wasn't in any position to voice a protest. Clearly a win-win.

"Do you have a lot of horses?" Tina asked.

"Yes. We have about fifty."

"That's a lot. I'd love to see them sometime."

Joe planted his right hand at the top of the steering wheel, using his arm to create a boundary between him and the brunette. "Maybe Celeste can bring you over."

Tina nodded and went silent.

Back in his younger days he would have made the most of a moment like this, because Tina was a cute and friendly diversion. He'd have his fun until things got a tad too serious, and then he'd move onto the next female.

Honestly, it had been his mom who had eventually called him out on his shit. She'd told him to quit acting like his father, always certain that heartbreak awaited. He'd been twenty-two years old when he'd finally learned what a tough

23

S.O.B. his grandfather had been to his dad, and how his mom had had to fight tooth and nail to get Buck Carrigan to let her into his heart. And somehow, in his childhood, Joe had acquired the same bad habit of never letting anyone get close to him.

Well, someone had—the half-drunk woman currently snoring with her face plastered against the side window—but he'd managed to push her far enough away that she apparently still hated him.

The snoring increased in volume and Tina shifted uncomfortably, but Joe couldn't hold back from laughing. "Let this be a lesson," he said.

"What's that?" Tina asked.

"Don't drink four Whiskey Sours."

He pulled up to a small house in a neighborhood and stepped out of the Bronco so that Tina could exit on his side. Skye never stirred.

Joe walked Tina to her door.

"It was really nice to meet you," Tina said.

He gave a nod.

"I guess I'll see you tomorrow?" She smiled expectantly up at him.

That caught his attention. Had he agreed to take her to the Mistletoe Ball? He didn't think so, but maybe Celeste had finagled it behind his back.

"Sounds good. Good night." He turned and headed back to his vehicle before she could question him further.

He'd call Ollie and set the whole thing straight. He'd let the man deal with Celeste. Even better, if Skye would agree to go with him, then he'd have a valid excuse to get out of whatever Celeste had cooked up.

He hopped back into his car and drove off without a glance in Tina's direction. Instead, he watched Skye in-between keeping his eye on the road. Her face had slid along the car window, causing her head to fall back. With her mouth now open, the snoring had taken on epic proportions. He chuckled. Not wanting to embarrass her, he flipped on the radio. "Dancing Queen" by ABBA filled the cab.

Perfect.

It was one of Skye's favorite songs. He remembered a Halloween party in middle school where Skye and Celeste had dressed up as the female members of ABBA and lip-synced the song. What had happened to that carefree girl?

With a loud snort, Skye bolted upright, suddenly awake. She looked at him, clearly confused.

"How was your nap?" he asked.

She ran the back of her hand along her mouth, wiping away the drool that had been glistening in the darkness. He suppressed a smile.

She looked around. "Where are we?"

"Almost to your folks' place."

She scrunched her face. "Where's your date?"

"She wasn't my date."

She pinned him with a suspicious glare. "Yes, she was. Any idiot could see that."

"Are you jealous, Skye?"

"What?" she scoffed. "Of course not." She turned away from him, gazing at the endless snow whipping by in a blur, and groaned.

"Are you gonna be sick?"

She responded with a hand over her mouth and another moan.

He pulled off the road and in seconds was out of the Bronco and grabbing hold of her just as she unloaded her burger and fries into a fluffy pile of snow. Shifting his stance, he held her up with one arm while gathering her hair with his other hand to keep it out of her face.

When the retching finally stopped, she clung onto him and came upright. "I'm fine. Thanks."

She stepped away, forcing him to break his hold on her.

"Sorry about that," she added.

"It's no trouble. But I know how you can pay me back."

"How?"

"Let's get back on the road, and I'll tell you."

Once he had her tucked back into the Bronco, he leaned across her and rolled the window down a crack. "The fresh air will help you from getting sick again."

"What's the payback? It's not like I actually puked in your car."

"And I greatly appreciate that. Why don't you let me take you to the Ball tomorrow?"

She snapped her gaze to him. "You want me to be your date?"

"Yeah. Why not?"

"Because Tina is your date."

"I don't want to date Tina. And you can help me get out of it."

"Oh. Right." She hiccupped. "That makes more sense."

"What are you talking about?"

"You're still a lowdown scoundrel, aren't you?" She shook her head, smothering another hiccup.

"Is that what you think of me?"

"Yes." Hiccup. "No." Hiccup. "Maybe."

He turned down the drive to The Quarter-Circle and parked in front of the main house. Before he had a chance to exit, she pushed the door open, stepped out and slipped, her arms flailing as she fell to the ground with a scream.

He quickly ran around the front of the Bronco, his feet sliding in all directions, but thankfully he had imbibed very little liquor and therefore possessed more dexterity, so he avoided a fall. Reaching her, he helped her to stand. "I think you need some coffee," he said.

"I'm fine, Carrigan. I've ice skated before."

"Is that what you call it?" But he didn't let go of her. Once she regained her balance, she ceased her struggle and locked eyes with him. Her hiccups had stopped, probably frightened into submission when she'd hit the ground.

"Why are you even more handsome now than back in high school?" She threw up her arms in exasperation, breaking his hold on her, and stomped away.

He held his breath, waiting for her to fall on her ass, but somehow she made it to the porch. Only then did he exhale with a big grin splitting his face. She thought he was handsome. He could work with that.

Gathering her luggage, he met her at the door. She opened the screen, gave a knock, then pushed open the main door. "Hello?"

"Skye?" Her mother's voice came from the living room.

Skye's father appeared from the kitchen, wiping his hands on a dishtowel he'd flung onto his shoulder. "Hi, darlin'. You made it. Did Ollie meet you?"

She let him draw her into a hug. "He did, but I got another ride."

Mr. Mallory caught sight of him. "Joey? It's good to see you."

"You too, sir." Joe deposited the suitcases along the wall of the foyer and shook the older man's hand.

Since returning to Durango, Joe had spent time with Oliver, but he'd only seen Mr. and Mrs. Mallory once. It still struck him how Griffin Mallory hadn't changed much in the past nine years—he was still tall and lanky, his dark hair streaked with the barest hint of white. The only thing age had changed was the deeper groove of wrinkles when he smiled.

"We haven't seen enough of you since you and Annie returned. Come on in and say hi to Livvy."

Joe slipped off his shoes and left them on the entry rug, obeying habits of old. Growing up, he'd spent a fair amount of time in this household, and Mrs. Mallory's rules were stamped in his head.

Skye popped off her shoes and hung her coat on one of the hooks that lined the entryway. As he shed his jacket, she darted around him, refusing to meet his eyes. The last time he'd been here had been with her. They'd spent two hours at the kitchen table eating Snickerdoodles, while Skye had tutored him in Trig and Physics.

He met Mr. Mallory's questioning gaze over Skye's behavior. "You might want to pump some coffee into her," Joe said quietly.

Skye's dad nodded with a knowing smile. "Got it. Can I get you anything?"

"No, I'm fine."

As Mr. Mallory headed back to the kitchen, Joe rounded the corner to the living room and was greeted by Olivia Mallory with a big bear hug. It never failed to surprise him how much Skye resembled her mom. "Joey," she squealed, patting his back, smelling of cinnamon and everything motherly and warm. "We're so happy that you and your mom moved back." She released him. "Come in and sit. How did you find Skye?"

While Skye and her mom sat on the couch, Joe settled into one of the stuffed chairs.

"She was at Hank's," Joe said. "I offered to drive her instead of Ollie. I'll get her car tomorrow."

A flash of panic crossed Skye's rosy-cheeked face.

"I had her leave it at Hank's," he added, covering for her, realizing she didn't want her folks to know about her little car wreck either.

"I can send one of the ranch hands to get it," Mr. Mallory said as he returned and handed a steaming mug to Skye.

"I don't remember asking for this," Skye said as she took hold of the cup.

"Have you been drinking?" Mrs. Mallory pinned her daughter with a glare.

Skye sank back onto the couch. "Just a little," she mumbled, and dutifully took a sip of the coffee.

"I can get her car with my Bronco," Joe said. "It's great in the snow. It's no trouble."

"You've still got that old thing?" Mr. Mallory laughed, sitting in the other matching stuffed chair. "You and Ollie sure spent enough time in it."

"Every few years, I've got to do something major to it, but it's hanging in there. I'm rather sentimental about it now."

Joe spent the next half hour catching up on old stories with Skye's parents, while Skye remained mostly silent, drinking her coffee and watching him over the rim of her Denver Broncos mug.

Sitting with the Mallorys, the flickering flames in the fireplace casting a soft glow around the room, Joe felt all warm and fuzzy inside. *Family.* He'd always felt that way here.

And then there was Skye. Her intelligence had always thrown him for a loop. As kids, he'd kept his distance, intimidated by Oliver's little sister. In high school, her drive and ambition had been tempered by her humor, and she'd become an annoying distraction to him—a girl unlike any of the others he normally chased, a girl who wasn't a quick fling, a girl that, frankly, had scared the hell out of him.

When he'd needed to get his grades up senior year or risk not graduating, his parents and her folks decided that she should tutor him, and he hadn't been able to get out of it.

Not that spending time with her had been a chore, but it only strengthened his resolve that despite wanting her, she was best kept far from his thoughts. And his heart.

He'd had plans after high school, and those plans had never included being tied down.

And then she'd gone and kissed him one night, confessing her feelings to him. In what he could only label a coward's move, he'd walked away and never looked back.

Until now.

He'd made a mistake then, but maybe he was getting a second chance.

"I'm trying to convince Skye to go to the Ball with me tomorrow," he said.

"Oh my gosh," Mrs. Mallory exclaimed, "that would be wonderful!"

Like a deer in headlights, Skye froze. "I don't have a dress," she said flatly.

"I might have something you could wear," Mrs. Mallory said.

Skye narrowed her eyes with a lethal glare directed straight at Joe. He held her gaze and tried not to laugh outright. Still a spitfire. Adult Skye was more captivating than any younger version had ever been. The minute she stepped out of her car earlier tonight, the past nine years had hit him square between the eyes. How had he said no to her that night? He must have been out of his mind.

But not anymore.

She turned to her mother. "No offense, Mom, but we're not quite from the same century."

"I'm not that unfashionable. And I've saved my wedding dress for you."

Skye gave a sarcastic snort. "Carrigan won't mind if I wear *that* tomorrow, would he?"

Mrs. Mallory tsked under her breath. "Skylar, I'm not your enemy."

"Sorry," Skye replied, looking contrite.

Mrs. Mallory said to Joe, "We'll figure something out. We'll make her presentable."

"I'm not worried," Joe said. "Skye always looks great."

Chapter Four

Still half asleep, Skye caught the scent of coffee and ambled downstairs. As soon as she entered the kitchen, she stopped short. Carrigan sat at the table shooting the breeze with her dad.

"Morning, sweetheart," her dad said.

She pulled the edges of her robe around her and cinched the belt tight. "Good morning," she mumbled, pushing her long hair behind an ear, wondering how unkempt it looked.

Carrigan watched her with an amused glint in his gaze.

She turned to the coffeepot and grabbed a mug to distract herself from how good he looked, all bright-eyed and bushy-tailed wearing jeans and a gray fleece jacket.

How could she be expected to face him at the crack of dawn?

It was bad enough he had infiltrated her dreams during the brief pockets of sleep she'd managed to grab, since her belly had cramped for much of the night with the swirl of coffee and whiskey dancing around for hours.

And she had a hazy recollection of snoring, vomiting,

and a supposed date to the Ball. She wasn't ready to face the memory of any of it.

"Joe towed your car back," her dad said.

Skye paused at the bread bag and glanced at the clock. *6:30 a.m.* "Already?" But it was a rhetorical question. She'd grown up on a ranch. If any sliver of daylight was present, then time was a wastin'. Except that it was December, and Joe must have hauled her car back in the dark.

Remembering her manners, which if she recalled correctly she hadn't practiced last night, she threw a thank you over her shoulder and went back to making toast. But the action made her realize she was still being rude.

Dammit. She paused and pinched her lips, then spun around. "Would either of you like something to eat?"

"I'm fine," her dad answered.

"I could use some eggs and bacon." Joe winked at her.

She suppressed a grimace. "Of course."

She went to the fridge and pulled out a carton of eggs, the butter dish, and a package of microwave bacon.

"I can't believe you drive a Prius," Joe said.

She set the food on the counter and grabbed a skillet from a low cabinet. "It's a company car."

"I guess you've figured out that fancy lawyer cars don't do well in the snow."

She slammed the pan onto the gas burner, wincing from the loud noise. "Environmentally-conscious ones are better for the earth."

"Well, those tiny city tires don't get any bite in the snow," he said.

"Thanks for the car lecture."

"He's right, Skye," her dad said. "I don't think you should drive it while you're here."

"Fine. Can I drive your truck?"

"It's in the shop."

"What about the truck with the feedbox?"

Her father looked at her as if she were six and had just fibbed about not leaving the chicken coop open. He wasn't buying it, and he hadn't then. Her mistake had cost six hens their lives when coyotes had hunted them down. Skye still felt terrible about it. She and ranch life had never been a good fit. When she had escaped to college, a weight had been lifted and she'd been able to breathe, finally free from the country life. Then why was the prospect of owning Mrs. Pendleton's ranch filling her with what she could only describe as excitement? Did she want a ranching life after all?

"Right," she said. "The cows need to eat more than I need to have transportation." She dropped a slice of butter into the pan and it started to melt. "I'll just ride Sarge whenever I need to go to town." Not that riding her favorite horse was a hardship. She issued a silent apology to Sarge for her sarcasm. *I'll bring you a few carrots as soon as I can,* she promised.

"I can loan you the Bronco." Joe stood and came to the coffee maker. As he refilled his cup, he bumped her arm. "I'll have mine sunny-side up."

She curled her lip and threw him an annoyed look. "I don't need your Bronco. I don't have anything pressing, just a meeting on Monday. I can borrow my mom's car." She had to peek around Carrigan's broad shoulders to see her dad. "Right?" she asked.

Her dad tilted his head in a skeptical nod. "Well, you'll have to work it out with your mother. You know how particular she is about her vehicle."

Skye cracked two eggs into the hot pan, and they crackled and sizzled. She waited for the other distracting sizzle to go back to his seat, but instead Joe stayed where he was and leaned against the counter, crossing one sock-clad foot over the other.

"I can drive you to your meeting on Monday." Joe sipped his coffee and looked down at her.

His nearness made her feel drunk all over again, and all she could do was shrug since her mind had blanked on a good retort. She needed to get out of the Ball first, and then she could focus on wiggling out of the next Joe-commitment.

Honestly, what was his game? If it were any other guy, she'd say he was flirting with her. But this was Carrigan, the guy who had steadfastly and completely ended any hope or idea of romance. Hell, she'd been so far gone back then that he could have seduced her, and she would have been a willing participant despite being only seventeen. And since it had been no secret that Joe had had a slew of girlfriends, rejecting her for sex had only crushed her more.

She pulled a packet of bacon from the box, placed it in the microwave above the stove, and punched in the time.

"You kids are gonna have to excuse me," her dad said, putting his empty coffee mug in the sink. "The animals expect breakfast too." He gave a squeeze to Skye's shoulder. "See you tonight, Joe."

"Yes, sir."

Skye transferred the eggs onto a plate, added toast and bacon, and handed the end result to Carrigan. She tucked a jar of strawberry jam under her elbow, and with her free hands took her coffee and a plate with her own toast and headed to the table. Joe joined her, sitting across from her.

"Thanks for breakfast," he said, smashing bread into yolk and taking a bite of the dripping mess.

Skye buttered her toast. "Don't you need to get back to your ranch and do ranch stuff?"

"I've got three guys working for us. I decided to take some time off this weekend."

She smeared jam on next and then took a bite. "How lazy for you."

"I need to have time to get myself presentable for the Ball."

She sighed. "Yeah, about that—"

"You agreed, Mallory. You can't back out now. And I've got another request. Ride with me over to the Pendleton Ranch."

She grabbed a napkin from the basket her mom kept on the table and wiped her fingers. "Why?"

"I need to ride the fence line and see what kind of shape it's in."

"That's trespassing." Although, technically, she was now the owner, so it wasn't. Still, the will would remain in probate for a while, so she'd likely not take ownership until January or February.

"Not if we stay on my side of the fence. The Triple C borders her property."

"Why do I have to go?"

He shrugged. "Just trying to be hospitable."

For the briefest second, she almost told him about the will, but she couldn't think of one reason to confide in him.

"Yeah, okay," she agreed. She should see the land that she now owned. The thought gave her a secret thrill.

"We trespassed when we were kids and didn't get in trouble then." He sat back, having finished his breakfast in record time.

His relaxed posture reminded her of those nights she'd spent tutoring him at this very table. She'd genuinely enjoyed being with him. His problem had never been his intellect but rather his focus, and she'd razzed him about it more than once.

"That didn't make it right," she said. "I'm a lawyer now. I can't willingly break the law."

"C'mon. Where's your sense of adventure?"

"Buried under piles of papers at work," she replied. But

suddenly she was sick of her attitude. Carrigan was turning her into a sour puss, and in the end, that's not how she wanted to be.

It was true that ever since she had seen him she'd had to contend with the familiar jolt that ignited every cell in her body. Side by side with that was the oppressive memory of his indifference toward her at the end of their friendship. But was that his fault? He couldn't help it if he didn't *like* her. He just liked her, in a nonspecific and friendly way. That was all. And he was trying to be nice now, trying to be her friend again. She needed to grow up and get over her school girl crush.

She popped the last of her toast in her mouth. "Fine. I'll just let my mom know that I'm heading out to commit a Class 3 Misdemeanor, so she's not surprised when the cops show up at her door." She stood. "Get the horses ready and I'll be right out."

His voice trailed after her as she headed to the stairs. "If we go to jail, I'll expect you to be my attorney."

As Skye rode beside Carrigan, her horse, Sarge, seemed rather playful with Joe's mount, a sorrel named Mr. Sunshine.

Since riding from The Quarter-Circle was too far with so much snow on the ground, Joe had decided they should load Sarge onto a horse trailer and bring him to the Triple C. When they arrived, Mrs. Carrigan had greeted her with a cup of coffee and a warm hug. While Joe got his and Skye's horses ready for riding, Skye spent twenty minutes reminiscing with Annie Carrigan.

"Your mom hasn't changed," Skye said, pulling her cowboy hat lower against a gust of wind.

"Thanks for visiting with her. I think she really enjoyed seeing you."

Joe twisted in the saddle and whistled. His two border collies, Ruby and Daisy, bounded through the snow.

Skye laughed. The crisp winter air combined with the powder blue sky put her into a festive mood. Soon there would be Christmas presents to open, church service to attend, and eggnog delights while watching "It's A Wonderful Life." She started singing "Jingle Bells" under her breath.

Two fluffy black-and-white tails swayed ahead of them as the dogs broke trail through the deep powder.

"Those two have so much energy," she remarked.

"Luckily they sleep as well as they play. They'll be passed out by seven p.m."

Skye indulged herself watching Joe from the corner of her eye. He was a cowboy right out of a romance novel—broad shoulders and a chiseled face beneath the shadow of his black Stetson. His gloved hand held the reins with a casual demeanor, and he moved with Mr. Sunshine as one unit. Taken from a purely aesthetic view, he was simply beautiful to watch.

"They take after you, then," she said.

"You think I'm in bed by seven p.m.?" White puffs of air came from his mouth as he spoke.

She allowed herself to smile. "No, I was referring to the *playing hard* part. Whatever happened to Penny Winston?"

"Beats me. I lost touch with everyone when I left."

"True radio-silence, huh? I guess I shouldn't be upset that you seemed to drop off the planet when your family moved north." She was proud there was no hint of the hurt in her voice. "You sure did leave a string of broken hearts behind," she added, letting Sarge pick his own path through the snowy field, since the terrain had become rocky and uneven.

"I think you're overestimating me. I was never serious about any of those girls."

Off to her right in the distance was the highway.

"We must be near The Peppermint Tree," she said, scanning the tree line beyond for a tall Ponderosa Pine bowed over at the top. When she caught sight of it, she frowned. "Why is your fence on the other side of it?"

"Because it belongs to me."

"What?"

He rode ahead, shutting down further conversation.

Mrs. Pendleton didn't own The Peppermint Tree? That was strange, because the old lady had loved that tree for some reason, having her ranch hands decorate it every Christmas. She halted Sarge nearby, dismounted, and walked toward the locally famous tree. But there were no decorations adorning the branches. This was likely the first Christmas in decades that it wasn't wearing its festive décor.

There had been times when snow would cling to its trunk in a pattern of stripes, as if there were heated coils insides, slanting in such a way as to look like a peppermint stick.

Stopping beside Joe, she removed her hat and craned her neck to look upward.

"Did you buy it?" she asked. "I can't imagine Mrs. Pendleton ever selling it."

He shook his head. "Nah. When I was in the process of purchasing the Triple C, a new survey was taken. The last one had been over a hundred years ago and true north had changed, thereby changing the property lines. The Peppermint Tree became mine."

"Huh. Mrs. Pendleton must've been crushed."

He sighed and adjusted his hat. "I'd describe it more as spitting mad. I think in her advanced years she'd lost her grip on reality."

"Really? I'm sorry to hear that. She was so nice when we

were kids. Do you mind me asking why you just didn't give it back to her?"

"Yeah, you're thinking I was being unreasonable to a senile little old lady."

She raised her eyebrows in response.

"The property line changed at about a thirty-degree angle," he said, "which sliced off this front corner, giving me The Peppermint Tree. But in the back, it cut right through Triple C land where the La Plata Springs was located."

"She got the water?"

He nodded. "I didn't really think I'd need it. There are other water sources on the property, but as it turns out, none this far west. And I was unable to tap into the water table anywhere around here. So, in the end, I really wanted access to that spring. I asked her for an easement, and in exchange I offered her full access to the tree."

"But she said no?"

"She did. Then she slapped me with a lawsuit, fighting for both the spring and the tree." He glanced around. "I'm not unreasonable, but she backed me into a corner. And then she died. So now I'm hoping to negotiate with the new owner, whoever that may be. You were close with her once. As near as I can tell, she had no children or immediate family. Would you have any idea who she left the property to?"

Yes. Me.

But the lawyer in Skye held back divulging this information. Until she could meet with Mrs. Pendleton's attorney and assess the legal aspects of the situation, it was imprudent to discuss this with someone with whom she was likely to soon be engaged in litigation. And màybe Mrs. Pendleton had a good reason to hold onto the spring.

She offered a shrug as her answer and sought to change the subject. "According to my mom, she and my dad shared their first kiss here when they were young and newly in love. And you and I met here."

"We did?"

"Well, we didn't meet exactly. I was eight. Ollie was supposed to watch out for me, so naturally he went prowling in the woods, and I was forced to follow. Actually, I didn't mind. I could've tattled and gotten him into trouble, but he let me tag along so I learned quickly to keep my mouth shut. I wanted to participate in his adventures. We'd heard so much about The Peppermint Tree and were naturally curious about it. When we got here, you were with three other boys."

"Now I remember," he said. "But who were the boys?"

"Stewie March, Henry Bennett, and Luke Greer."

"How do you remember that?"

She smirked. "I'm blessed with a knack for remembering useless minutiae, but it comes in handy at my job. Those three boys started giving Ollie a hard time. I was shocked because I'd never seen my brother in an underdog position. He generally bossed me around any chance he got. I was a little afraid, so I hid." She nodded toward the thick trunk. "The Peppermint Tree offered me a good hiding place. But you stepped in and protected Ollie. After that, you two started hanging out together. I remember thinking at the time that you were a very fair person, and it was my first inkling that I wanted to study law, to help the underdog. Aside from my dad, you were always the best boy I knew."

When she caught him staring at her, it was clear she'd spilled too much. Dang it.

She started walking around The Peppermint Tree, avoiding his gaze.

"I was like every other boy growing up," he said. "Sometimes good, sometimes bad."

"And sometimes ugly?" she teased, disappearing behind

the trunk. The Peppermint Tree had a wide girth, wider than what was normal for a pine tree.

She popped around the side suddenly. "Boo!"

Carrigan jumped. "What the hell."

"Did you think I'd disappeared?" She grinned. "I used to do this to Ollie. One time, I convinced him that I'd gone to a secret place. I really had him going that this tree is steeped in magic."

Carrigan's gaze was on her again, watching, scrutinizing, and for a moment she couldn't breathe.

No. No way was she falling for this again.

Stepping back, she broke eye contact. "We should get back to the horses."

Then she fled.

Chapter Five

Skye put the finishing touches on her roast beef sandwich, adding sliced tomato, lettuce, onions, and Muenster cheese. She slathered mustard onto the bread and placed it atop the masterpiece, then cut it in two with a large butcher knife.

The front door opened and shut with a slam, and Ollie entered the kitchen, bundled into his work coat and still wearing his cowboy hat. He went straight to the fridge and started drinking directly from the milk jug.

Skye carried her plate and a glass of ice tea to the table, and said, "Does Mom know you break every house rule you can?"

He walked over to the table. Skye had just set the plate down when he snatched half her sandwich.

"Hey! That's mine!" She tried to grab it back, but he took a big bite then held it away from her. "And your boots are still on," she added. "I'm so telling on you."

He kicked the chair out and sat. "What are you? Twelve?"

Skye grunted, grabbed a chip bag, and dropped into her seat. She spread a nice pile of salty potato chips onto her plate to make up for the missing part of her sandwich.

Her morning escapade with Carrigan had left her hungry, in more ways than one, but she was determined to be a grownup about it.

Beyond the kitchen window, the world had taken on a somber hue with overcast skies and the start of more snow falling. It was going to be difficult to get into town and find a dress. She bit into her sandwich and let her shoulders slump with a sigh.

"Why are you so glum?" Ollie asked.

"Do you think I'd look good in Mom's wedding dress?"

He shrugged, wiping his mouth with his sleeve. "How should I know?"

How had Ollie already finished his half of her sandwich?

"Haven't you ever seen a photo of Mom and Dad on their wedding day?" she asked.

He shook his head as he chugged more milk.

"It's hanging on the wall in the hallway," she said, her voice rising in exasperation with each enunciated word.

"I never noticed." He offered the jug to her.

She curled her lip in protest. "Gross."

Suspicion overtook his gaze. "Are you getting married?"

"No. I need a dress for the Mistletoe Ball."

"You're going?"

"Yeah, with Carrigan."

Ollie knocked his hat up an inch and stared at her, his silence all but crackling between them.

Skye frowned. "Why are you looking at me like that?"

His gaze softened. "I don't profess to know anything about anything when it comes to your love life, but you sure moped around when Joe moved away years ago. Maybe you should steer clear of him."

Ollie's admission surprised her. She hadn't realized anyone had noticed, least of all her brother.

"Thanks for your concern," she said, "but this isn't a real date. We're just going as friends."

He considered her explanation for a second, then said, "That'll make Celeste happy, at least."

"It will?"

"She's kinda been trying to fix Carrigan up with her friend Tina."

I knew it.

Skye drowned her sorrows by jamming a chip in her mouth. To shift the focus to a different topic, she asked, "When did you and Celeste start dating?"

"We're talking about your love life, not mine."

"So? She's my best friend and you're my brother. I have a right to know."

He stood and carried the milk to the fridge. "I'm not talking about this. But you should call Celeste."

"To ask her about you?"

He shook his head. "No. To tell her that you and Carrigan are just friends."

Right. Because everyone should know about her non-romantic status with the man of her dreams, especially her oldest and dearest friend.

Ollie walked out of the kitchen, the front door opening and closing as he departed the house.

Skye held her cellphone to her ear. "Do you have a dress I can wear?"

Celeste answered with her own question. "Are you and Carrigan a thing?"

"No, of course not. Why do you ask?" Skye sat on her

bed in her old upstairs room and looked out the window, watching the horses in the corral as they munched on hay.

"Because he just called me and said he was taking you tonight as his date," Celeste said, her tone strained.

"I'm not his date. We're just friends. He's just being nice by taking me."

"Really?" Celeste's mood brightened. "Because I've been working the Tina angle for over a week now."

"No worries, I've got no claim on Carrigan," Skye said, trying to sound like she really meant it, but her belly did a full-on somersault in revolt.

Celeste sighed loudly, clearly relieved. "Okay, good. I'm glad to hear it. As for a dress, I doubt I can help you. You're bustier than I am."

"Is that shop on Main still open?" Skye scratched her head a little too vigorously, dislodging the messy bun that was holding her hair at bay.

"I know the one you mean. Hang on. Let me call them."

Skye examined her fingernails, wondering if she would have time for bit of polish. She'd already dismissed the notion when Celeste came back on.

"It's closed because of weather," she said. "Maybe the Ball will be canceled too?"

"It's possible," Skye conceded. That would keep her from being seen in public wearing her mother's wedding dress, while arriving on the arm of Carrigan only to hand him off to Tina.

Man, how did her life manage to suck so much?

"You didn't bring anything from Denver to wear?" Celeste asked.

"It didn't cross my mind that I'd need a cocktail dress."

"Why *did* you come early for the holidays?"

Skye needed to tell someone, so she decided to come

clean. "Mrs. Pendleton's attorney sent me a copy of her will."

"Why?"

"Because she left me something."

"Oh my gosh," Celeste squealed. "Did she leave you her doll collection?"

Celeste's response took Skye aback. She had no idea that her friend was so passionate about the display Mrs. Pendleton had kept in a glass case in her living room.

"No." Skye dragged the word out. If the collection came with the property, she made an impulsive decision to give it to Celeste. "She left me her ranch."

Several seconds of silence on the other end, then Celeste said, "The whole thing?"

"Yep."

"What? Wow! Why would she do that?"

Skye switched her phone to her other ear. "I really don't know. But I have a meeting with the attorney on Monday. That's why I came home at the last minute."

"What are you going to do? Sell it?"

"I don't know. But don't tell anyone for now. Okay?"

"Sure. Of course."

"And speaking of secrets, when were you gonna tell me about you and Ollie?"

Celeste gave a nervous laugh. "Please don't be mad. I wasn't sure in the beginning how it was going to go, and I didn't want to jinx it by talking about it. Believe me, if I thought you could help me with your bullheaded sibling, I would've let you know, but you're more of a liability than an asset in this particular love connection."

"True. Ollie has never heeded my advice in the romance arena."

"The heart wants what it wants."

"And how is it going?"

"I really like him, Skye," Celeste said, her voice sounding dreamy.

"Then I'm happy for you."

"I'll let you in on another secret—I've liked him since we were kids."

Welcome to the club. Maybe she should tell Celeste about her years-long crush on Joe Carrigan, but at this point the entire subject seemed moot.

Thankfully, Celeste changed the subject. "Did you check the closet in your old room? Maybe you left something behind that you could wear tonight."

Skye went to the closet and flipped the light on. The walk-in was the best feature of this room, and she'd begged her parents to let her have this oasis when she was five years old, even though Ollie was older. Her mom had been using it as a guest room until that time. This was the biggest bedroom besides the master and by all rights, the eldest child should have had it. But Skye's begging had finally worn them down, and in spite of Ollie's grumbling—this room was better located to the stairs and hence had made sneaking out of the house better; even at a young age Ollie had been cognizant of this feature—they let her have it.

Tucking the cellphone against her ear with her shoulder, she began to flick through the clothes, the rhythmic scraping of hangars signaling her progress. A lot of it was obviously her mom's because Skye was certain she would never wear red paisley or a magenta sweater decorated with sequins. Hiding in the back, however, was something covered in a plastic bag. Grabbing it, she headed to the bed and laid it out.

She switched her phone to speaker and tossed it onto the bedcovers.

"I think I might have found something," Skye said.

"Yeah?" A crunching sound came from Celeste.

"What are you eating?" Skye untied the knot in the plastic bag at the bottom and pushed it up to reveal a blast from the past.

"Carrots. Why?"

Skye eyed the treasure she'd just unearthed. "You've always had such good snacking habits."

"Thank you." More crunching.

"I found my prom dress." Skye unhooked the tight burgundy number from the hangar and held it against her chest.

"Oh, wow!" Celeste stopped her munching. "I loved that dress. You looked so pretty that night."

Skye almost blurted out that when she'd bought it, she had been thinking about Carrigan, had secretly harbored a fervent hope that he would return, admit he'd been a fool the year before, sweep her off her feet, and take her to her Senior Prom, despite him already having graduated. Instead, she'd finally accepted Mark Anderson's offer because he'd been the only one still allowing himself to be strung along at the eleventh hour.

Celeste started eating again. "Okay, so don't take this the wrong way, because you look freaking awesome these days, but … do you think you can squeeze into it?"

Skye twirled back and forth before the long mirror hanging on the back of her bedroom door, trying to determine if it would fit. The irony wasn't lost on her that she would finally be able to wear it for the male she'd had in mind when purchasing it.

"Give me a sec so I can get it on," Skye said.

She searched her suitcase but soon realized she'd only brought one bra with her, and it wasn't a low-cut lacy one, but rather a practical, tan-colored one meant to be worn underneath a t-shirt. More digging through her clothes only turned up a somewhat tattered sports bra.

"Damn," she said.

"What's wrong?" Celeste asked.

"I don't have the right bra."

"If I'm remembering right, isn't the bust already tight? I'll bet you could get away without one. How about pasties? Do you have any?"

"Do you really think I thought to bring those?" Skye disrobed, dropping her shirt and jeans onto the bed.

"Maybe your mom has some." Celeste slurped loudly.

"Ugh. I'm not asking her that. And you're a very noisy eater, by the way."

"Sorry. I skipped breakfast."

Skye shimmied into the dress and was only able to zip up the back halfway. She eyed herself. She was showing a bit more cleavage than when she was eighteen, but maybe it could work. Besides, it would serve Carrigan right to be forced to look at the luscious swell of her bosom all night. She snorted at the thought.

"What's going on?" Celeste asked.

"Hang on." Skye grabbed her phone. "I'll take a pic and show you." She snapped a selfie in the mirror and texted it to Celeste.

Twenty seconds later, Celeste cooed. "Oooo, it looks good, girl. But what about shoes?"

Skye went back into her closet and searched the floor and shelves for shoeboxes. After flipping the lid on several, she found the original black heels she'd worn with the dress. Jamming her feet into them, she wobbled as she walked back into the bedroom.

"I can still get my feet into my high school heels," she said.

"For real?" Celeste exclaimed. "You're lucky. I'm pretty sure I'm a whole shoe size bigger than my teenage self."

"Well, it's tight. I don't have any pantyhose though."

"It's all right. Hose are out for now unless you're in the royal family."

"I know, but it's arctic out there."

"Hey, nobody said being a woman was easy."

Chapter Six

*C*arrigan took the porch steps two at a time, opened the screen decorated with a Christmas wreath, and knocked on the Mallorys' front door, which opened seconds later.

Mr. Mallory greeted him, wearing a coat and tie. "Joey, you look great."

"Thank you, sir. You too." Joe stepped inside. He had on the nicest suit he owned, the one he'd worn to his father's funeral. He hadn't imagined he would have another opportunity to wear it again so soon, but maybe it was for the best. Losing his dad had been a turning point in his life, and now it felt like Skye might be a part of that shift as well.

As he was driving over, nerves had gripped him. What if Skye backed out?

He had tried to call her to let her know that the Ball hadn't been called off due to weather, in case she had assumed it was, but it had gone straight to voicemail.

Mr. Mallory waved him into the living room. "No, don't take off your shoes. Livvy is a bit neurotic about that, but it's more that she doesn't want horse and cow shit in the house. I'm sure your dress shoes are fine."

Joe nodded and decided to leave his black wool coat on as well. With hope, Skye wouldn't make him wait too long and send him into overheat mode. "Do you and Mrs. Mallory want to ride with us?"

Skye's dad shook his head. "Nah. You kids head on over. We might want to leave early, and we wouldn't want to cramp your style."

"I'll be careful on the roads," Joe assured him.

"It stopped snowing two hours ago, and I'm sure the plows are out clearing the way. But if it gets late and the roads seem icy, then stay put. Don't risk it."

"Yes, sir. I'll take care of her." Joe hesitated. "Is she here? I wasn't sure if she still wanted to go."

Mr. Mallory chuckled. "She's upstairs. Shouldn't be long now."

Skye's mom breezed into the room, wearing a black gown trimmed with red, her graying hair pinned away from her face.

"You look beautiful, Mrs. Mallory," Joe said.

She giggled and patted his arm. "Thank you. It's fun to get dressed up. And I love that the event benefits the women's shelter. You cut quite the figure, Joey." She added in a low voice, "You and Skye make such a great couple."

He didn't know what to say. The attention shifted to the stairs at the sound of heels tapping on wood. Skye entered and halted abruptly.

There was a pregnant pause while everyone froze in their positions.

In high school, Skye had been on the tomboyish side, her frame more athletic than voluptuous, but it was clear that the ensuing years had rounded out those burgeoning curves. She looked stunning in a maroon dress, revealing an ample swell of her breasts. He flicked his eyes back to her face, aware that he'd been staring.

His mouth went dry. It was like he'd never seen a woman before.

"Is there something wrong?" Skye asked.

"Is that your old prom dress?" Mrs. Mallory's question caused Skye's face to pinch into a grimace.

"It was all I could find on such short notice."

Her makeup accentuated her already creamy complexion, and the dark lipstick put Joe in mind of a temptress.

Bewildered, his mind went blank.

"Shall we go?" she prompted.

He cleared his throat, snapping out of his stupor. "Let me start the Bronco," he said, feeling a little tongue-tied, "so I can get the heat going." The double innuendo hung in the air as he headed out the door.

Damn. He was in trouble.

BUNDLED into her mom's wool coat, Skye held her hands up to the nearest vent as Joe drove onto the highway in the day's draining light. The snow was cleared from the roadway and shoved to either side into high berms.

She sighed as the chill in her fingers abated. Her feet were comfy and toasty in a pair of snow boots—she planned to change into her heels once they arrived at the country club.

Skye tried her best not to look at Joe. She'd never imagined he could clean up so well. He was a cowboy through and through, but in his black suit with a blue shirt and festive tie, he appeared like something out of a James Bond movie.

For a moment she indulged the fantasy that they were about to dive into danger and romance, and her heart pounded in anticipation.

"Who'd you go to prom with?" Joe asked, his jaw set in a hard line.

"Mark Anderson."

"Anderson?" He threw her a surprised glance.

"Yes. So?"

"Skinny Anderson?" He had the nerve to laugh.

She watched the road. "He was slender."

"I heard a gust of wind blew him off his horse once."

She shook her head. "Don't be ridiculous."

"You know what his life motto was, right?"

Forcing herself to look at Carrigan, she waited with an expectant expression for him to further criticize her high school dating choices.

"When in doubt, chicken out," he said.

She frowned.

"So did he?" Carrigan continued.

"Did he what?"

"Chicken out at prom."

Understanding the implication, she pressed her lips together. "Don't be crude."

His dark demeanor suddenly shifted to dazzling charm as he grinned. "He did chicken out," he said.

She crossed her arms. "That's none of your business." The memory of Mark's fumbling attempts to kiss her at the end of the evening surfaced, making her feel bad again that she'd rejected him. She'd had no interest in Anderson, or any high school boy, beyond friendship, but she wasn't about to admit that to Carrigan.

"How about college?" Joe asked. "Anybody serious?"

"I had boyfriends, if that's what you're asking."

"But no one current?"

"Maybe," she hedged. "I meet a lot of men in my profession."

That didn't come out right. It made her sound like a prostitute. Carrigan's cheery countenance downshifted into a glower.

"But no one serious," she added, though she had no idea why she would throw Carrigan a bone, except that his mood swings were giving her whiplash. "I'm sure you're never lonely," she muttered, looking out the window as she spoke in case she hadn't sufficiently hidden her despair over his rejection of her nine years ago. She didn't want him to see it in her eyes.

"I made some mistakes in high school," he admitted.

You don't say.

"I should've taken you to prom instead of ..."

Skye glared at him. Did the man seriously not remember who he took to prom? "Sara Neville," she supplied through gritted teeth. Unfortunately, she remembered every girl he had been tied to during his four years at Durango High. "You went to junior prom with Pam Oleander."

"Oh, yeah. Now I remember. I put sex appeal over friendship."

And there it was.

"You were a good friend, Skye, and I'm sorry I trampled over it."

She couldn't believe it. She knew she was in the friend zone, but did he need to point it out like an ugly blemish on her face?

"Can we listen to the radio?" she managed to say before her throat closed and tears threatened to ruin her makeup. She returned her gaze to the passing scenery of trees and snow.

So much for thinking she could handle being his friend.

He switched on the music, and to the steady beat of "Satisfaction" by the Stones, Skye contemplated how quickly she could get out of this evening.

Chapter Seven

Joe escorted Skye into the ballroom at the San Juan Country Club. A festive atmosphere greeted them along with several Christmas trees decked out in ribbons, ornaments, and pine cones. Colorful lights adorned the walls and dinner tables surrounded a dance floor, while Bing Crosby crooned "White Christmas."

Skye headed straight for the bar on the far side, and Joe struggled to keep up with her, surprised at her speed considering the heels she wore. He had hoped to catch her under the mistletoe in the lobby, but she blew right past it.

"Can I have a gin and tonic?" she ordered.

He leaned an elbow on the counter and looked at her profile. "Since when do you drink gin and tonics?" For a nanosecond, he indulged a glance at her cleavage, then he turned to the bartender. "Whiskey neat."

She arched an eyebrow. "No beer for the cowboy?"

"I'm not always a hick, Skye."

Her prickly demeanor confounded him. Something had happened during the car ride, but he had no idea what. Or why she was acting so standoffish.

Ollie and Celeste appeared looking well-dressed in formal attire, Celeste's green dress dazzling when it caught the light. Tina was right behind her, hanging back. Joe ran a hand behind his neck. Damn. In her modest black dress, she wasn't an unattractive woman, but *mousy* kept running through his head.

He'd been hoping that Celeste had taken the hint when he'd told her that he was taking Skye tonight, but the implied message hadn't gotten through because Celeste somehow maneuvered Tina to his side, and the woman gave him an uncertain smile.

Apparently he needed to be more forthright.

But he didn't want to be rude either. "You look very nice, Tina."

"Thanks."

"Can I get you a drink?"

"A white wine would be nice."

He stepped away to place the order, noticing out of the corner of his eye that Skye was now speaking with a tall man on her right. Jealousy flashed through him.

Ollie came up on his left and said quietly, "You and Skye make a striking pair."

Joe was taken aback by the frosty glare Skye's brother gave him. He wasn't sure whether to be relieved that someone finally realized how he felt about Skye or laugh because her brother looked about ready to challenge him to a fight.

Grabbing his whiskey, Joe took a drink, then said, "I think you should tell Celeste."

Ollie narrowed his gaze. "And what exactly should I tell her?"

"That this is a real date with Skye." Joe finished his drink and gave a nod for another.

Ollie gave a snort of disdain. "That's not what Skye told

her."

They'd managed to keep their conversation private, but when the bartender placed the white wine on the counter, Joe couldn't ignore Tina any longer. He returned to her and handed her the drink, as Ollie gave a frozen concoction to Celeste.

"Who's that talking to Skye?" Joe asked.

"That's Mark Anderson," Celeste said. "He went to high school with us."

The man's ears must be burning, considering that Joe and Skye had been talking about him earlier. While annoyed that Skye's attention had shifted so completely to another man, the saving grace for Anderson was that he appeared to have a date at his side, a woman Joe didn't recognize and to whom Skye was speaking with equal congeniality. He wondered if Anderson recognized Skye's dress, the very one he'd probably tried to finagle her out of all those years ago.

Skye was far too alluring in that old prom gown, and no doubt Anderson was reliving the last time he'd seen her in that dress, current date or not. Joe contemplated shedding his jacket to cover Skye's distracting attributes.

"What are your plans for Christmas?" Tina asked him.

Reluctantly, he turned his attention to the mousy woman. "I'll spend it with my mom."

"It'll be the first one without your dad," Celeste said. "I'm sure it will be difficult for you both. Tina will be headed out-of-town."

"And where's that?" Joe asked, keeping Skye in his line of sight.

"Albuquerque."

"I thought you were from Dallas."

"I am," Tina replied, "but my dad lives in New Mexico now."

"You'll be driving?" He'd emptied his second whiskey, so

he set the glass on the counter. He planned to have a clear head tonight, not something he'd always practiced in high school.

Tina nodded. "Yes. It's not too far. Hopefully these storms will stop."

"One of my ranch hands is also headed that way," Joe said. "His name is Kyle. Maybe you two can drive together."

"Sure. I'll give you my number," she added, a little too enthusiastically.

Shit. She'd misread his suggestion, which was that Kyle was single and possibly better suited for her.

A waiter approached and asked if everyone would be seated for dinner, saving Joe from sticking his foot in his mouth any further. Skye—still chatting with Anderson and his date— moved away from him, and it was crystal clear she had no intention of sitting with him.

"Excuse me," he said and quickly stepped away from Tina, Ollie, and Celeste.

He returned to the bar, ordered another gin and tonic, then carried the excuse to Skye and her new tablemates.

He handed the drink to her. "I thought you might need a new one."

She glanced at him in surprise. "Thanks." Her voice held all the enthusiasm of thanking the dentist for a root canal.

"Joe Carrigan?" Anderson stood and reached out a hand. Shaking it, Joe said, "It's nice to see you again, Mark."

"Are you here with Skye?"

"Guilty as charged." Joe took the cue to grab the seat beside his date, whether she acknowledged it or not.

Skye wrinkled her brow and said under her breath, "I figured you'd be sitting with Ollie and Celeste and your *girlfriend.*"

"I'm not the kind of guy to abandon my date," he replied quietly, although Anderson was no longer paying attention to either of them since the waiter was depositing a basket of rolls onto the table.

"We both know I'm not your date."

Joe leaned close. "That's where you're wrong, Skylar."

"Joe," Anderson said, turning back to him. "I'd like you to meet my wife, Paula."

It was the best news he'd heard all night. Smiling broadly, he rose slightly from his seat and reached over to clasp her hand. "It's a pleasure to meet you."

SKYE WAS HEADED TO THE LADIES' room when Celeste caught up and hooked an arm with hers.

"What's going on, Skye?" she asked as they made their way into the bathroom lounge.

"What do you mean?" Skye sank onto one of the couches and popped off her painful shoes, then wiggled her toes.

"Carrigan didn't leave your side all through dinner. What am I supposed to tell Tina?"

"I have no idea," she replied wearily, leaning her head against the cushion and closing her eyes. She was as confounded by Carrigan's behavior as Celeste, and she was reaching her limit of friendly small talk with the man. It only made her want him more.

She considered confiding in Celeste her true feelings, but it would put her friend in an awkward position because of Tina.

Someone burst into the lounge. "Skye, why didn't you tell us?"

Her mother.

Skye cracked an eye open. "Tell you what?"

"About you inheriting the Pendleton Ranch." Olivia Mallory stood with hands on hips.

Skye cast a condemning look at Celeste.

"I didn't tell," Celeste exclaimed. "I promise."

"Mrs. Archibald told me," her mother replied. "She knows someone who works at the courthouse, and you of all people should know that when a will enters probate it can be viewed by the public."

"Oh, yeah." Skye sat up and started jamming her feet back into her shoes.

"Is it true?" her mom asked.

Skye stood. "Yes."

Her mom's gaze softened. "That's incredible. I can't believe Charlotte would do that."

Skye reached out to squeeze her mom's arm. "I know. I'm still a little stunned by the gesture."

"What are you going to do?"

"I'm not sure yet. I'm meeting with her attorney on Monday."

"So that's why you came down out-of-the-blue?"

"Yes. I just learned of it a few days ago."

Her mom paused, giving her a knowing look. "You're thinking of keeping it, aren't you?"

And that was the truth of it. Skye didn't just want to manage the place; she wanted to move in and make a life here. At first, she thought her ambivalence over the decision was because she'd be living next door to her folks, but that wouldn't be a hardship. In fact, it would be kind of nice.

No, the crux of the issue lay in the fact that the Three C also bordered the property. Joe Carrigan would be her neighbor.

Damn the man.

Now what was she supposed to do? Bear witness while he married and had a houseful of little Carrigans?

Frustration pushed her temper to a boiling point. When had she become one of those women who let her life be dictated by the whims of a man? Who the hell was Carrigan to keep her from coming home if that's what she wanted?

Goddamn the man.

Chapter Eight

*J*oe scanned the crowded dance floor. Where was she?

A merry melee of couples crowded before him, tuxedos and gowns of various lengths all meshed together beneath a flashing disco ball.

He caught sight of Tina three tables over. He spun around and headed in the opposite direction, and spied Skye at the bar.

He came up behind her and leaned his mouth close to her ear. "You can't keep avoiding me."

She jumped. "My God. You're so quiet. What are you? An assassin?"

"Just a cowboy. How about a dance?"

She didn't exactly agree but didn't resist when he placed a hand on her lower back and guided her to the dance floor. Once they infiltrated the throng of couples clinging to one another as they swayed to Frank Sinatra, Skye turned to him, her face a blank mask. He folded her hand into his and wrapped his other arm around her, enjoying her proximity.

Spending time with her hadn't unfolded as organically as he'd hoped, since she'd managed to avoid him for large chunks of the evening.

"Did seeing Anderson make you feel like you were at prom again?" he asked, trying to ignore the cleavage teasing his senses and the heady scent reminding him of wildflowers.

She shrugged. "He's doing well, of which I'm glad, and his wife is very lovely."

She wouldn't look at him, her countenance as icy as a frozen lake.

"Am I missing something here?" he asked.

"I'm tired. I want to go home."

"I was hoping to spend some time with you."

Putting distance between them, she raised her chin and locked eyes with him. "Are you now? What a piece of work you are, Carrigan."

Her anger ignited the small space between them.

"Why do you say that?" He pressed his hand against her back to keep her from walking away, because one thing was certain—she was about ready to bolt.

"I'm tired of being at your beck and call." Her voice seethed in a furious whisper. "You rejected me all those years ago, and now you're just stringing me along again. You can't have it both ways. You can't keep treating me like some consolation prize and expect me to put up with it."

Taken aback by her outburst, he attempted to regroup. "I'm not stringing you along."

"I can't do this anymore." She tried to leave again, but he held fast to her. "I can't be your friend," she bit out, her voice still lowered so as not to attract attention. "I've tried. It's too difficult."

The shadow of pain in her eyes brought him up short.

He'd had no idea how much he had screwed up until this instant.

He grabbed her hand and led her out of the ballroom as Brenda Lee started singing "Rockin' Around the Christmas Tree." His grip firm, he wasn't about to let her go. At least not until he said his piece. He continued through the well-lit but mostly empty lobby, weaving around a couch and chair.

He continued down a hallway toward the men's locker room.

When she realized his intent, she stopped and yanked on his hand. "Where are we going?"

"Trust me." He pushed open the door and peeked inside. "All clear."

They needed privacy, and it was too cold to go outside.

Country club restroom facilities were nothing if not spacious. He took her through the lounge and pulled her around the corner to a dark side hallway, out of view should any gentlemen enter, and positioned her against the wall.

He looked down at her. "I need to explain something," he said, his lips mere inches from hers. "That night when you kissed me—"

"We don't need to relive the past."

He placed his other hand against the wall, boxing her in. "I told you that night that I wasn't interested."

Her eyes flashed. "I know. I was there."

"It wasn't the truth."

She cast her eyes downward, pinching her lips in an angry line.

"I did want you, Skye," he admitted. "But there were so many reasons why it wasn't a good idea."

"I'm so glad we're clearing this up." She tried to leave but he pressed closer, stopping her.

"You were my best friend's sister, I was about to move away, and I didn't want to treat you like the other girls."

"You mean the ones that you *did* kiss."

He stared at her mouth. "And you were so out of my

league," he admitted, the truth slipping through the last of his defenses against her. He had never admitted this to anyone, least of all himself, until this moment.

"You don't have to justify to me why there was no spark between us."

He cupped her face with his hands. "There was most definitely a spark and now it's a full-blown inferno, and I'm done being careful around you."

SKYE STOPPED breathing as Carrigan's mouth crushed hers, his breath hot and his lips hungry. He tasted of whiskey and his skin smelled of aftershave, and her body and willpower succumbed quickly. She'd spent years dreaming of what he might taste like, how his cheeks would feel beneath her fingertips, and now that it was here she wasn't going to waste a minute.

She slid her fingers into his hair and pulled him closer as his tongue made a clean sweep of her mouth. Her body arched against his, wanting to be as close to him as possible.

His arms wrapped around her and his hands pressed her hips against his arousal, sending rockets of pleasure clear down to her toes. He strengthened his assault with his mouth and her knees buckled. She hung onto him as if she were sliding off a cliff.

The wall bumped her from behind as he kissed her again, soundly, his hands palming her buttocks, and she nearly came right then. She tore her mouth from his to catch her breath, to somehow get this fire under control, but Carrigan's demanding lips went to her neck, sucking and biting as he headed south. Lust flashed through her like wildfire.

Carrigan wanted her. And she had *always* wanted him.

Good God. There was no doubt in her mind that she was about to have sex standing up in the men's locker room.

She grabbed onto his shoulders as his mouth and hands tortured her breasts through the fabric of her dress. Her breath came in ragged gasps and she moaned.

His face came to hers again. "Skye." The heat in his voice wrecked any remaining defenses she might have had against him.

Her breath mingled with his. He held her face and gave her another deep, devastating kiss. With her body trembling, she took hold of his jacket and yanked it from his shoulders.

Male voices beyond startled her, and Carrigan broke the kiss. He leaned over her, protecting her, while Skye sought to remain quiet as her chest heaved up and down as if she'd been sprinting.

He rubbed against her as his lips trailed down her cheek, sending delicious shivers through her, her breasts reacting to the contact despite the clothing separating them.

Carrigan's mouth came to her ear. "I don't have any protection," he said, his voice husky and full of need. And regret.

She reached up and raked her fingers down his cheek, then ran her thumb across his lower lip. "It's alright," she whispered. "I've got it covered."

She'd remained on contraception out of habit, although it had been many weeks since the last unremarkable encounter with Dingbat Dave. But now, she was glad for her attention to routine. She didn't want anything to stop what was about to happen between her and Carrigan.

He kissed her slowly, quietly, since they weren't alone, as his hand cupped her breast.

Another upwelling of pleasure threatened to cascade right out of her body.

If Carrigan kept this up, she'd cross the finish line before he even had her undressed. Thankfully, his mouth absorbed the groan that almost escaped her throat. Then his lips moved to her jawline, her neck, her collarbone, and back to the swell of cleavage now barely contained by her old dress.

She ran her fingers through his hair again, clutching onto him.

The men finally left, and Skye released a gasp, having held it in check while Carrigan had managed to wrench the dress down from her shoulders, exposing her breasts, and he'd gone to work silently torturing each nipple with his mouth.

But the more he tugged, the less she could move her arms, the gown becoming a straitjacket, leaving her breasts exposed as if on display at a buffet, flushed and glistening from Carrigan's attention.

"I want you," she said, "but I can't move."

He paused, his face buried in her bosom, and looked up at her, his gaze wild and unfocused.

She tried to raise her arms, but she was like a Tyrannosaurus rex with tiny, useless limbs.

He stood and tried to return the dress back to its original position, but her breasts stubbornly refused to pop back into the fabric where they belonged.

"Wait," she said and turned slightly. "Try to release the zipper."

He tugged and jerked and then tugged again, but it wouldn't budge.

"You'll have to break it," she said.

"Won't that ruin the dress?"

"I think you've already managed to do that." She readied herself. "Go ahead."

She swung her girls, perky and alert, away from his view because he couldn't seem to take his eyes off them.

"I'm not sure we should ruin your dress," he uttered, his lips on her shoulder. "How will I get you out of here looking like this?"

"Very carefully," she said over her shoulder. "You could tell everyone I'm a stripper."

Carrigan's deep chuckle only made her nipples pucker more. "You'd sure give those old codgers something to talk about tomorrow."

With one hard yank, the zipper gave way and the dress released, now hanging at her waist. His hands came around her and pressed her backside against his very prominent arousal. She braced her hands on the wall as another wave of desire slammed into her.

"You look even better than you did in high school," he whispered, his breath hot against her ear.

His hands moved upward, and she shuddered.

Panting, she leaned her forehead against the wall. "We need to be quick."

"Are you sure about this?" he asked, holding her against him. He bit the skin along her neck, igniting gooseflesh.

"Yes."

Although the zipper on her dress was now open, it was still jammed at the bottom, making it impossible for her to push it past her hips. It was just as well. Standing completely naked in the men's locker room probably wasn't a good idea. She hiked the skirt up, then hooked her thumbs in the waist-band of her panties and in one motion she gave Carrigan full access.

He rested a hand on her bare bottom. "Don't move," he growled.

She peeked over her shoulder as he dropped his pants, and then she leaned back against him. It was delicious and exciting, a dream that she'd had for so long that she could hardly believe it was happening.

"Skylar, you're killing me," he hissed.

She arched her back to make it easier for him. He paused and pushed slowly to join with her.

Damn his restraint.

Impatient, she made a backward thrust and captured the complete length of him.

The locker room door opened again, and once more two men entered, chatting with each other.

Carrigan went still. As she tried to remain unmoving and silent, her leg muscles began to burn. Carrigan shifted slightly and one hand grasped a breast while the other went south, and she was forced to sink her teeth into her forearm to stop the cry that was clawing its way from her chest.

He began to withdraw and reenter slowly, and she closed her eyes, trying to keep her release at bay, at least until they were alone again.

She heard the faucet go on and off, and finally the men's voices faded as they exited into the hallway and departed.

Please no more interruptions.

Carrigan didn't waste any time. He thrust hard, and on the third one, he had her. His arms gripped her in a vice as his own violent release overtook him, and she rode the waves that rocked her while reveling in his response.

Awash in the primal aftermath, Skye's thoughts were swimming in a haze of ecstasy. She rested her forehead against the wall as she sought to regain her breath.

Every nerve ending in her body was humming, and when he withdrew from her, she was still too blown away to do anything but hold up the wall.

"Stay put." He disappeared into the bathroom.

Skye glanced down at herself and almost laughed at her appearance.

Carrigan had really done a number on her dress, but in

her high heels her wantonness was rather heady. At least she could now check sex kitten off her to-do list. She had begun to worry that she was destined to be a stodgy lawyer for the rest of her life.

With shaky hands, she repositioned the lower portion of her clothing and then looped her arms into the sleeves and held the fabric over her chest.

Carrigan reappeared, his pants secure and his blue shirt tucked right where it should be. But the wicked grin he gave her put her in mind of a rogue pirate instead of a well-dressed cowboy. He handed her a moistened hand towel.

"Thank you." But she couldn't perform a proper clean-up on herself with only one hand free, and truthfully, she didn't want to remove Carrigan's mark from her just yet. "But what I really want is a pizza. I think you knocked out my blood sugar." So much for witty after-sex banter.

He stepped behind her and took hold of the gaping backside of the dress and was able to secure the hook at the top, but the zipper was uncooperative. "I'll give you whatever you want, Skye, but first we're going to have to get you out of here without ruining your reputation." He ran his fingers along her still exposed back, and she shivered. He pulled her hair to the side and gave her a quick kiss to her exposed neck. "I think this dress is done for."

He picked up his coat, shook it out, and draped her in it.

She faced him.

"You ready to go?" he asked, gripping the lapels and pulling her to him for a kiss.

She sank into it, her hunger for him hardly satisfied and hooked an arm around his neck and feasted on his mouth until he came up for air. His readiness pressed against her leg.

"Let's get out of here," he said.

"Can you grab my purse? It's at the table where we had dinner."

"Got it." He stood back. "Let me make sure it's clear before you leave." He kissed her once more, then went to check the locker room exit. She peered around the corner, and he waved her forward. She moved quickly and soon planted herself on the couch in the lobby.

"Be right back," Carrigan said.

———

JOE MADE his way to the table where he and Skye had sat earlier and quickly retrieved her small clutch. Then he headed to the coat check and grabbed both of their coats.

Since he had every intention of taking her back to his place, he knew he needed to alert Skye's family. Luckily, he crossed paths with Ollie.

"Skye's having trouble with her dress, so we're leaving," he said.

Ollie raised a skeptical eyebrow. "And I'm sure you had nothing to do with it."

"Can you tell your folks that she's with me?"

"Let me guess—you're not taking her home, are you?"

Joe didn't say anything.

Ollie shook his head and waved him off. "Fine. I don't want to know any more."

"Will you tell Celeste, so she'll get off my case about Tina once and for all?"

Ollie grimaced and nodded. "She's gonna be very annoyed with you and Skye." Then, he added in a sarcastic tone, "I appreciate that I get to deliver this news. There's a good chance my evening just went south."

"Sorry about that." Joe clapped him on the shoulder. "I owe you."

As he left the ballroom, Ollie's voice trailed after him. "You owe me twice."

Skye was still sitting where he'd left her, her face flushed and looking damned pretty, and a heady anticipation filled him. He wanted her again, as if the locker room had been only foreplay.

He took her hand and helped her stand, then blocked her from the ballroom crowd as she slipped off his dinner jacket, the seductive curve of her bare back flashing him as he replaced it with her wool coat. He led her outside and a cold blast of air hit them, rocking her on her heels. Since they were alone, he scooped her into his arms.

"In case you weren't swept off your feet before," he said, carrying her to his vehicle.

"No chance of that, Carrigan," she murmured into his ear.

He grinned and tucked her into his Bronco. As he drove, he pulled her across the bench seat to sit beside him then flipped on the radio.

"Since you like music so much," he teased, referring to her earlier request.

She leaned her head on his shoulder. "I was a little mad at you."

"Yeah, I noticed."

He kept his hand tucked between her knees except when he used the stick shift, enjoying the feel of her skin. For a while, they drove in silence, and he imagined getting her alone in his bed.

He passed the turnoff to her folks' ranch.

She lifted her head. "Where are we going?"

"My place."

She cleared her throat. "No offense, Carrigan, but I don't think we should be frolicking all night long with your mom in the next room."

He shifted his hand higher on her thigh, and she gave a quick intake of breath.

"Relax," he said. "I didn't get a chance to give you a tour earlier, but I live in the guesthouse. I love my mom, but I do need my own space. I am a grown man after all."

"I noticed. I didn't realize the Triple C had two houses."

"It's small, but it'll do for now."

"I can't stay all night," she said. "What about my parents?"

"I had Ollie tell them."

"Tell them what?"

"That you're mine for the night."

She frowned. "Seriously?"

He smiled. "No. But I did have him say that I left with you. And I told him to set Celeste straight, too."

"About Tina?"

He nodded.

Skye groaned. "Celeste will be pissed at both of us."

"She'll get over it."

He took a left onto his property, stopping the Bronco in front of his small house. Skye scooted away and switched her heels for the snow boots she'd brought with her. He hopped out and came around to help her from the vehicle. Holding her hand, he led her up the stairs and opened the front door.

Ruby and Daisy greeted them with tails wagging. He pushed past them to get inside, and Skye knelt to give them both a proper hello.

"Oh, you sweet girls," Skye crooned, laughing as both mutts slathered her cheeks with doggie kisses.

"All right," Joe said. "You three can have a lovefest later." He loosened his tie, then reached a hand out to Skye and pulled her to her feet. "Right now, you're the only female allowed in my bed."

"Is that an invitation?"

He brought her close and kissed her. "Definitely."

"I accept." She smiled down at her competition. "Will they try to push me out?"

Still holding her hand, he headed upstairs. "Not if we can shut the door quickly."

Chapter Nine

*J*oe awoke the following morning alone in his bed, sprawled on his stomach. As last night's events replayed in his mind, swift desire gripped his body, and he debated calling Skye on her cellphone and begging her to return to his bed. She had insisted on leaving before dawn so she wouldn't worry her parents. Or let them catch a hint of her wanton behavior. Those had been her very words. He'd chuckled then—and smiled now—because as far as he was concerned, she could practice her wanton behavior on him anytime she liked. But he'd done as she asked and had driven her back to The Quarter-Circle.

He glanced at the clock. It was already after seven a.m. Damn, he'd overslept, but then he hadn't had much slumber during the night.

Her scent lingered on the sheets, an early Christmas present that he hadn't realized he'd wanted or needed. But Skye was in his blood. She always had been. He'd wasted the last nine years—he didn't want to waste another day.

He reached for his phone on the nightstand, unplugged the charging cord, and punched in her number.

"Hello," came her sleepy response.

"Good morning."

"Hmmm."

He propped his back against the headboard, ignoring the chilled morning air on his bare chest. "When can I see you today?" He had chores waiting, but he'd get through them as fast as he could.

Muffled sounds filled his ear as she likely shifted her pillow.

After a second, she said, "Well, when do you *want* to see me?"

"You could help me feed the cattle."

"Sounds like a lot of work," she said, sounding as if she were snuggling deep under the covers.

"I forgot. You don't like ranching."

"Now hang on." Her voice gained in strength. "I could be convinced."

"How?"

"Buy me dinner?"

He sat forward and ran a hand through his hair. Ruby and Daisy took notice from their position at the foot of his bed and peeked at him over the edge, tongues wagging and tails thumping on the wooden floor. Once Skye had left, they hadn't taken their usual roost in bed with him. He hoped they weren't feeling neglected.

"How about you come here, and we'll eat with my mom?" Not the most ideal way to woo a woman, but he wanted to keep all the females in his life happy. Besides, if Skye were going to be in his life—and he hoped she would be —better sooner than later to get his mom on board.

"That would be nice," she replied. "Let me get a shower, and then I'll come over."

"You can shower here. And I'll make you eggs and coffee for your trouble."

A husky laugh was her response. "My parents will never believe that I got up so early to do ranch work."

"There's always a first for everything."

A pause and the barest hint of a sigh from her end.

"Skye."

"Yeah?"

"Look, I'm sorry about what happened nine years ago. I shouldn't have done that to you. I could've been nicer. I could've stayed in touch."

"Are you developing a conscience, Carrigan?"

"Would it get you back in my bed?"

"I can say with resounding certainty that getting me into bed is the least of your problems."

He grinned. "I like the direction this is headed."

"Give me fifteen minutes." Then she hung up.

SKYE SPENT the entire day with Carrigan. First, he whipped up breakfast in his surprisingly well-stocked kitchen. Turns out he could cook. It was eggs and bacon not only for her, but Ruby and Daisy as well. If Skye had had a tail, she would have been wagging it in glee right along with his smitten canines.

Then, he made good on his offer to let her shower at his place, hopping in to join her. Skye wasn't sure how clean she was at the end of it, since they ended up back in the bedroom after. While staying naked and warm all day beneath a blanket with Carrigan held great appeal, he did have ranch work to do, so she put her hair in a ponytail and joined him.

They moved feed out to the cattle, checked water troughs, and tended the horses before finally joining Annie Carrigan for dinner at the main house of the Triple C.

"It smells wonderful," Skye said, yanking off her snow boots before giving Mrs. Carrigan a quick hug.

Annie Carrigan's short gray hair and slim, sturdy figure gave her an air of efficiency, but when she smiled, her mouth stretched wide, and she had the look of a young girl. Skye had no doubt that Buck Carrigan had been unable to resist her, and Joe had the same star quality.

"It's Joey's favorite—Sloppy Joes," Annie replied.

"I always thought they were named after me," he said, hanging his hat on a wall hook and shucking his work jacket.

Soon they were sitting around the small kitchen table, food piled high on Skye's plate. All the hard labor today had left her famished, and she'd grabbed generous portions of baked beans and Mrs. Carrigan's homemade potato salad.

"Normally this is a summer dinner," Annie said, pouring ice water from a pitcher into a glass and handing it to Skye. "But I try to make it at least once a week for Joe."

"He's lucky to have you," Skye replied.

She waited while Mrs. Carrigan blessed the food, then they all dug in.

"Where are those dogs of yours, Joey?" his mom asked.

"I left them at my house. I figured they'd be obnoxious and disrupt dinner."

"They're my little darlings. Would they have bothered you, Skye?"

She shook her head, then added around a mouthful of food, "Not at all."

"See?" Annie said with a satisfied tone. "Your dogs aren't going to scare her away."

Carrigan went still, his cheeks getting red, then slowly resumed his eating without looking at her. His mother had obviously embarrassed him, and his endearing reaction made Skye smile.

"The Triple C is a nice property," Skye said, taking a drink and setting her glass down.

"Yes," Annie agreed. "We're settling in, but I imagine that Joey will try to find more land. I think he wants to make an offer for the Pendleton property, once we can figure out who took ownership since the poor woman's death. Although it's hard to have sympathy for her. She's been difficult with Joe these past few months, and years ago she was difficult with Buck."

Skye had been on the verge of confessing that *she* was the new owner, when she stopped and cleared her throat. "Why? What happened?"

"Oh, it was probably twenty years ago or more," Annie said, "but every time we wanted to do something regarding fencing or signage, or even how many trees we were allowed to remove from our property, she argued against it in the town hall meetings. It wasn't just us—she had very specific ideas of how land should be handled, and she wanted everyone to side with her. Well, Buck could be a bit ornery, especially when it came to a woman telling him what to do. When she could, Mrs. Pendleton went the legal route. Quite frankly, that woman was a nuisance. And then there was that damned Peppermint Tree."

She stood and gathered their now empty plates. Skye popped out of her seat to help.

"I know there were a great many of us who made pilgrimages to the tree," Annie said as she went to the sink. "I don't think she realized how many there were."

"Yeah, we got away with it more than once." Joe stood and poked his head into the refrigerator. "Any dessert?"

"There's cake on the counter." Annie nodded to a pan covered with foil.

Joe made a beeline for it, grabbing a fork out of the silverware drawer.

"And you didn't get away with it," Annie added. "Mrs. Pendleton complained to everyone about you kids, including the police. It's to your father's credit, and yours," she said, glancing at Skye, "that kept you kids from getting into trouble."

Skye took the dessert plates that Mrs. Carrigan handed her and carried them to the table. With guilt simmering just below the surface, Skye let the moment to confess slide past, determined that once she could understand all the legal squabbles that Mrs. Pendleton apparently had been embroiled in, she would try to make everything right.

The chocolate cake was delicious, but Skye couldn't enjoy it. She had thought that inheriting the property would be a good thing, but now she was beginning to have doubts.

After dinner, Joe went outside with her, his warm hand engulfing hers as they headed toward his house.

"I think I should go back to my folks," she said. "I've been away all day. They're gonna think something's up."

He stopped to look at her. "Something is up."

She smiled and kissed him. "Besides, I drove here in my Prius. I'd better get back before it gets dark and the roads are bad."

"All right. Drive carefully. You still want me to take you to that meeting in town tomorrow?"

"No, I'll be fine."

"It's no trouble. I've got an appointment, too."

"I may have other errands to run for my mom. But can we meet after?"

Once she knew the details of the inheritance she wanted to tell Joe everything.

"How about lunch at that diner on Main?"

She nodded. "I'll be there."

Chapter Ten

_S_kye studied the paperwork that Brian Fogle, Mrs. Pendleton's attorney, had handed her. They sat at the end of a long table in a conference room, not unlike the one at Skye's firm.

"As you can see, we need to settle a few things in regard to the estate before you can take possession," Mr. Fogle said, adjusting his glasses, his shock of white hair combed back from his face.

Skye nodded. "I'll look at these more closely on my own," she said, indicating the pile he'd given her of assets and debt owed. She stifled a yawn. Legal work could be a bit dull even on a good day, but with her current lack of sleep— all thanks to Carrigan—she really could use a nap.

"Can I ask you something?" she asked.

Mr. Fogle nodded.

"Why did Mrs. Pendleton leave it all to me? To say that it was a surprise is an understatement."

"Well, that leads me to the next issue. There's pending litigation on the property."

"I'm aware of the boundary issues with the Triple C. Are you saying she left me her estate because I'm a lawyer?"

"I think it has more to do with the fact that you're a Mallory. Do you also know about the grazing leases?" He cleared his throat and reached for a glass of water the receptionist had left on the table.

"No."

"In the last few years, Mrs. Pendleton had reduced the stock on her land and had offered leases to her neighbors, The Triple C and The Quarter-Circle."

This was news. Skye was surprised her folks hadn't mentioned it, but then Skye hadn't expressed much interest in the finer details of ranch life. Until now.

"When Joe Carrigan bought the Triple C," Mr. Fogle continued, "he also acquired the current leasing terms, but Mrs. Pendleton wasn't happy with him and decided to break the lease."

"She was unhappy about the boundary dispute?"

"That was part of it. But it seems she had a history with the Carrigan men. A few decades ago, she'd fought for grazing rights against Joe's father, Buck Carrigan, and it left a bitter taste in her mouth. I'm guessing she dislikes Joe by association. Anyway, Joe filed a breach of contract against her."

This echoed some of what Joe's mother had said last night at dinner.

Skye frowned. "You mean separate from the boundary issue?"

"Yes."

"Does he have a case?"

"I don't know the particulars. A different lawyer was handling it for Mrs. Pendleton." He rifled through his papers, extracted one, and handed it to her. "Here's his information. You should contact him directly."

Skye nodded, wondering why Joe hadn't brought it up.

"It was during this time," Mr. Fogle continued, "that Mrs. Pendleton drew up a will."

"She didn't already have one?" Skye asked, surprised.

"It was odd, but no, she didn't. She spoke about you and how she'd always thought of you as a daughter, how she had always thought highly of your family. It's my belief, and I could be wrong, that because Mallory property also abuts hers, she sought to protect the land from a grubby Carrigan getting his hands on it." He glanced at her, his gaze sheepish beneath bushy white eyebrows. "My apologies. Those were her words."

Skye nodded. "I see."

Wouldn't Fogle love to know whose bed Skye had been warming recently? But that was her business.

She knew enough about contracts and negotiating that until she did her due diligence and read through everything, she couldn't make an assumption on Carrigan's guilt or innocence in the matter between him and Mrs. Pendleton.

She didn't want to believe that perhaps he'd taken advantage of an old lady in declining health, but unfortunately, that could happen. And despite Mrs. Pendleton's many bad traits in dealing with the community in the past few decades, the fact of the matter was that she had entrusted Skye to do right by her property.

And Skye would do just that. If Fogle's calculations were correct, the land and the house was worth about three million. There was no mortgage or active liens.

Had Carrigan known about the inheritance before he'd dragged her into the men's room at the country club? She didn't think so. That would mean he'd been lying to her all this time. But hadn't she deceived him as well by not telling him that she owned the property?

Skye gathered the documents and put them in her briefcase, then pushed her chair out and stood. "Thank you, Mr. Fogle."

He shook her hand. "I'll be in touch as things progress. Since you don't live in town any longer, I'm guessing that you'll want to sell the property. I can put you in touch with a good realtor."

As they walked out of the conference room and down the hallway, she said, "Actually, I'm not sure what I'm going to do, but I'll let you know if I need a contact."

They rounded the corner to the reception area and Skye stopped abruptly. "Joe?"

Carrigan was seated on one of the couches but shot to his feet when he saw her. "Skye." His brow furrowed. "Was this your appointment? Did you have lawyer business?"

"Of a sort."

"Do you both know each other?" Mr. Fogle asked.

Joe's gaze made her heart skip a beat. "You could say that," he said.

Skye turned to Fogle. "Yes, I'm sorry I didn't mention it during our talk." But why was Joe here? Especially after the way Fogle had described Mrs. Pendleton's assessment of the Carrigan men?

"Well, then this might mitigate our meeting, Mr. Carrigan," Fogle said.

"And why's that?" Joe asked.

"Because the new owner of the Pendleton property is Ms. Mallory."

Surprise crossed Carrigan's face. "You're kidding."

"I'm afraid not," Skye replied.

JOE WAITED until the waitress placed two cups of coffee on

the table before addressing the giant elephant in the room. Skye didn't seem in any hurry to talk.

To say he was shocked that Skye not only had inherited the Pendleton Ranch but also had neglected to tell him was an understatement.

"Have you known the whole time you've been here?" he asked.

She added cream and sugar, avoiding his gaze. "Yes."

"Why didn't you tell me?"

She took a sip of her coffee and shrugged. "I didn't really tell anyone."

While their relationship was new—barely off the ground, really—it still stung that she hadn't confided in him.

"Why did she leave it to you?" he asked.

She started to speak, then appeared to dismiss it, opening her mouth again only to furrow her forehead. She almost looked in pain.

"To be honest, I really don't know," she finally said. "Our families were always on friendly terms and I genuinely liked her when I was young, but I hadn't seen her in a while." She took another sip of her coffee. "It would seem that the disagreements between you and her pushed her to finally make a will."

"And name you the beneficiary?"

Skye narrowed her gaze and jutted her chin. "Apparently, she was never fond of you Carrigans. Your mother certainly confirmed that last night."

"And she thought you would protect the land from me?" This whole thing was becoming more bizarre by the minute. "Skye, I never had a grudge against the woman."

"Did you file a lawsuit for broken grazing leases?" Her eyes held a glint of accusation.

"Yes." He frowned. "Look, if you think I was trying to indiscriminately hurt a little old lady, you're wrong. But she was wrong to break the leases. Did your dad tell you that she also broke his leases?"

"No."

He scrubbed a hand across his face, then rested his arms on the table. "Probably because shortly after, she reinstated his but not mine. I filed the lawsuit to protect my interests. I was more than willing to negotiate with her, but she wouldn't even talk to me. And then, near the end, she really wasn't of sound mind. I was very sorry that she died, but I went to Fogle's office today to find out who the new owner was so that I could talk to *them*. Which I guess is *you*. I'm willing to forgive you for not telling me. So, can we try to resolve this?"

"You're willing to forgive me?" Skye said. "I didn't owe you an explanation. To be honest, this was none of your business."

"Like hell. We're more than friends now."

She took a deep breath. "Look, until I have a chance to look through the paperwork that Fogle gave me, I can't discuss this with you. And we shouldn't … continue our relationship. Because it's distracting and a little unethical at this point."

"Wait." His head was spinning. "It's not like I committed a crime. We can still see each other. This is crazy, Skye."

Her cellphone rang. When she looked at the caller ID, her face pinched in clear frustration. "It's work. I have to take this." She answered the call. "This is Skye."

Whoever was on the other line did the talking while Skye nodded, voicing a litany of *yes sirs* until she finally hung up.

With her face taut, she said, "I have to go back to Denver."

"Now? I thought you were here until Christmas." Her business-like demeanor was putting distance between them, and he didn't like it.

"I'm in the doghouse at work. It's a long story."

"And you don't want to tell me about that either, do you?" He hadn't meant to sound so bitter, but it grated along the edge of his voice anyway. "Tell me something. If I hadn't run into you at the attorney's office this morning, were you going to tell me about the will?"

"Yes. I was going to talk to you today after I'd spoken with Fogle. I wanted to understand what was going on first."

"You could've asked me."

"I feel an obligation to do the right thing." She chewed on her lower lip then released a deep breath. "Look, give me a few days to study the situation and assess the legal problems."

A sense of foreboding that had hung over him in high school resurfaced. It had been why he'd stayed away from her all those years ago, because deep down he'd always felt that Skye was too good for him.

And she had just treated him as such.

It wasn't going to work with her, was it?

Pain sliced through him.

He committed to memory the blue of her eyes, the curve of her lips, the elegant contours of her neck. She was more beautiful than he had ever remembered. In the instant he'd learned she had inherited Mrs. Pendleton's property, a rush of elation had hit him, because it meant that maybe, just maybe, she'd return—permanently. She could live here, right next door to him, until he could convince her to live *with* him.

Because, God help him, he wanted her for more than a casual fling.

But he'd always known her ambition would take her far from Durango. And in his heart, he was a rancher. Even when she'd tutored him back then, trying to give him a leg up on his future, he'd yearned for a simpler and quieter life.

Nine years ago, he'd had the strength to walk away from her.

Now, he had to do it again.

His heart screamed mutiny, but he ignored it.

He was a cowboy. He'd always be a cowboy.

"When are you leaving?" he asked.

"Today."

"Then you'd better get going."

Chapter Eleven

"*He* won't take my calls." Skye shifted her cellphone to her other ear and leaned back on the plush couch, tugging a blanket atop her. It was December 23 and blustery weather howled outside her Denver condo.

"According to Ollie," Celeste said, "Joe has been a real bear since you left. I think the man misses you. Maybe he's mad that you lied to him about the inheritance during your whirlwind weekend, and he's upset you're not taking his side on his problems with Mrs. Pendleton."

Skye had shared the events of the past two weeks with her best friend, finally confessing everything to her—about the Pendleton property, the litigation, her wild few days with Carrigan, and her issues at work.

"I didn't lie. Not exactly." But maybe Celeste was right. She should have told him.

The crinkle of a wrapper could be heard on the other end.

"What are you eating?" Skye's own hunger drove her curiosity. She'd been working long hours to help her firm finalize a deal with a new client out of San Francisco, and she'd been running herself ragged, knowing she had to prove herself to make up for the Dave-debacle.

"A candy cane. Just getting into the spirit. Listen, from everything you've told me, two things are clear. You hate your job, and you want to be a ranch lady. Oh, and you're in love with Carrigan. I guess that's three things."

Skye sighed. Celeste spoke the truth, about all of it. "When did you become so wise?"

"It's a gift," Celeste teased.

"I'm worried that Joe will feel pressured by my moving back, as if it's for him. He's already rejected me once. What if this drives him away completely?"

"Okay, look. Your voice lights up when you talk about the potential for Mrs. Pendleton's property. I think she left it to you, because she knew that you were the best one to take care of the land. So, take ownership and definitely *own that ship*. As for Carrigan, you need to talk to him, face to face. Get your butt down here. Now!"

"I'll come tomorrow," Skye said.

"Great! I'll see you Christmas Day. Ollie invited me to The Quarter-Circle for your mom's famous ham."

Skye ended the call and rose from the couch with renewed purpose. She headed to her bedroom to pack.

———

EMOTION FILLED Skye as she entered Mrs. Pendleton's modest ranch house, a wave of stagnant air and misuse greeting her. It was as she remembered it with the antique furniture, the large collection of horse artwork that the older woman had favored, and the Native American trinkets displayed in glass cases. There was also the doll collection. She'd have to get Celeste over here after the holidays to have a look at it. Mr. Fogle had informed Skye when she'd stopped by his office on her way through Durango that the house contents—as well as any farm and ranching equipment—belonged to her.

Regret washed over Skye. She hadn't tried to visit the elderly woman when Mrs. Pendleton had gone into assisted living after injuring herself slipping off a bottom stair step. And then the dementia had set in at a frighteningly fast rate. Although, considering the trouble Joe had had with her, her faculties likely had been in decline much sooner.

We never have enough time.

A lump formed in Skye's throat as she walked into the kitchen with its rustic oak cabinets and homey feel. A large window overlooked an idyllic meadow, creating a peaceful scene.

It was Christmas Eve, and Skye envisioned future Christmases here—a fire blazing in the hearth, pies baking in the kitchen, and the sound of children.

Skye couldn't help but smile.

She wanted this.

A home, a ranch, a life.

With Joe.

She hoped …

She had called him this morning, but it had once again gone to his voicemail. She'd left a message, telling him she was driving down and asking if she could stop by The Triple C later. While his radio silence was reminiscent of the pain of his rejection from long ago, she refused to think that this was the end. If she had to, she'd squat in his house until he was forced to talk to her.

But first, she needed to come here, to be sure this was what she wanted.

And it was.

Now, no matter how her meeting with him went, she could stand strong in her decision to take possession of the

Pendleton property. This was the direction she wanted her life to take. If it didn't work out with Joe, then she would keep her chin up and go on. She'd done it before. She could do it again.

Skye ventured into a room serving as an office with a large, dark-stained desk. Dust coated the banker's lamp and pencil holder, along with a blank tablet of paper. She walked slowly around the solid piece of furniture, admiring the heavy wood and numerous iron accents, which looked hand-forged. She pulled the top right drawer open and was surprised to see a photo album resting inside that she had made for Mrs. Pendleton.

She lifted it out and began to flip through the pages. It had been a handmade Christmas gift that Skye had crafted during high school, after Mrs. Pendleton had confided in her about losing her husband in a car accident long ago and her great sadness over never having had any children of her own. Wanting to give the dear woman a sense of family, Skye had shared the only one she had by making an album of her and Oliver.

Once again, Skye fought back tears that Mrs. Pendleton had kept the gift all this time, ultimately returning the gesture with a present far more grandiose.

Skye glanced upward. "Mrs. Pendleton, you win when it comes to Christmas gifts," she whispered. "I promise I'll take care of this place you called home for so long."

She was about to close the book when her gaze stopped on a photo of two boys and a girl—Ollie, Joe, and her. She was probably about ten years old, her hair pulled into a ponytail and her grin showcasing crooked front teeth before orthodontics had given her a better smile. She was hanging on a fencing gate beside Ollie and Joe. Only a year older than her, they were scrawnier versions of themselves. Skye marveled that her mom had allowed Ollie to sport such a ridiculous mop of shaggy hair, and Joe's skinny arms protruding from a striped t-shirt bore no resemblance to the man's solid physique today.

The front door opened, startling Skye, and she peeked into the foyer. Joe stepped inside, his cowboy hat in his hand, and wiped his boots on the rug while looking at her.

"I saw the Prius," he said and gave a shake of his head. "You've really got to stop driving that in the snow." He shut the door.

At the sight of him, her heartbeat doubled its tune, putting the Little Drummer Boy to shame. She stepped into the foyer.

"Hi, Carrigan. I was beginning to think I needed to send out smoke signals to get your attention."

He stared at her for a moment. "Why did you come back?"

For you, you big lug. Oh, sweet Santa Claus. Was he really going to make her beg?

"Because I told you I would," she replied, her back stiffening as her irritation climbed. "I haven't been happy at my job for some time, so when I learned that I'd inherited all of this, my initial reaction was excitement. It seemed as if the guy upstairs was telling me that I should come back. And deep down I wanted to. But then I ran into you, and within one day you turned my world upside down."

"I don't understand. What are you saying?"

He remained rooted to his spot on the entryway rug, so Skye stepped closer to him.

"I'm moving in," she said. "And if you can't handle it, then I'm sorry."

His dark eyes clouded with confusion. "Why would I not be able to handle it?"

Skye planted her hands on her hips. "Because I'm guessing you think I'm putting pressure on you."

"Pressure for what?"

"For you! For us!" She threw up her hands. "We'll be neighbors. And if our relationship has already crashed and burned, then we'll be forced to watch the other one shack up with somebody else."

His face downshifted from stone-cold granite to fiery beast. "Like hell," he grumbled. "If anybody's shacking up with you, it's me."

"Then why haven't you returned *any* of my calls?" Her voice hitched and she nearly sobbed.

He took a step toward her. "I didn't want to hold you back, Skylar. I'm always going to be a rancher, and I didn't want to force you into a life you didn't really want. I've always known that about you. I knew it the night you kissed me back in high school. You were always headed to the big city."

"But what if I want to come back?" she asked quietly.

"Then I'll hold onto you and never let go."

"Promise?"

He nodded. "I promise."

She moved into his arms and kissed him. As her mouth consumed his, her anxiety finally abated. He did want her. He hadn't turned and run.

The taste of him ignited her hunger and a burning need to get him into bed.

"It's much too cold to fool around in here," she murmured against his mouth. The electricity was shut off and a sharp chill permeated the house.

"When has location ever stopped us before?" His hands slipped underneath the edge of her tweed peacoat and dived into the waistband of her pants.

When his icy fingers reached her flesh, she squealed. He laughed, and she stepped back to regroup. Joe leaned down to pick up his hat, which he'd lost hold of after she'd thrown herself into his arms.

While getting naked with Carrigan made her think all kinds of wicked thoughts, she wasn't quite ready to do the boom-boom in Mrs. Pendleton's house.

"I think I want to clean the place out a bit, put my own touch on it, before you knock me off my feet again."

"Compliments will get you everywhere, Mallory. But I get it. We can mattress-dance at my house, if you like."

"Such a way with words, Carrigan." Then, she added, "You never asked what I've decided about the litigation."

"Because it doesn't matter. I'll give up on all of it, if it means causing strife between us."

"What?" she said, aghast. "No! If I were your lawyer, I'd advise against it. Look, I studied everything, and Mrs. Pendleton was clearly in breach of the leasing contracts, so I'll honor them. And I'll grant you access to the La Plata Springs. But I do have one condition."

"Anything," he replied.

"Will you give me an easement to The Peppermint Tree?"

"I'll do one better," he said, lacing his fingers with hers. "I'll reset the boundary line and give ownership back to you. It should stay with this property anyway. I think that's why Mrs. Pendleton gave it to you. She knew you would make the peace and do right by the land."

"She managed to see what I couldn't for the longest time."

"What's that?"

"This is where I belong."

He tugged her close and murmured against her lips, "It's where we both belong."

Chapter Twelve

hristmas Eve
One Year Later

JOE WAITED IN HIS BRONCO, the vehicle pulled off the highway idling. Luckily, the massive storm that had been forecast earlier in the week had yet to make an appearance, and it was the only reason he had let Skye drive back from her business in Albuquerque today. Otherwise, he would've had her stay put.

Not that he didn't want to see her but chancing a replay of her road-slide from a year ago didn't sit well with him.

Thankfully, she only traveled occasionally now for the legal work she continued to do. She negotiated land contracts for an associate who'd offered her a job when she had decided to leave Denver and her firm. But mostly, she managed the Pendleton Ranch. Her parents had gifted her fifty Black and Red Angus, and she had acquired six horses. And while Joe generally didn't help her with the day-to-day —Skye was determined to do it herself—he did send two of his ranch hands over twice a week to keep her workload manageable.

Joe was just happy to have her close—and in his bed. It hadn't been easy for her, juggling a ranch, part-time lawyering, and renovating Mrs. Pendleton's house.

But now he was ready to officially help with the workload by merging their properties. He was ready to put a ring on it.

The radio cranked out "Rudolph The Red-Nosed Reindeer" as he picked up his cellphone and punched in her number. On the second ring, she answered.

"I'm almost there, Carrigan."

"Good. Is that you I see coming down the road?"

"Is it? Where are you?"

He smiled. "Notice anything?"

She gasped. "The Peppermint Tree!"

He'd had to get a cherry picker to decorate the damned thing because it was so tall, and he'd spent two days splicing into an electric panel at a nearby well pump so he could run an extension cord, but he was rather impressed with the result. In the waning daylight, the colorful lights glowed, giving off a festive air. He half-expected Santa to appear from behind the giant trunk at any moment.

Skye had suggested the tree was magic. Surely anything was possible. Finding Skye again was proof of that.

She guided her Subaru hatchback, far superior in the snow than her Prius—which her firm had reclaimed—and stopped her vehicle in front of his. She hopped out grinning.

He ended the call and stepped out of his Bronco, patting his chest to reassure himself that he still had the jewelry box tucked into an interior pocket of his work coat. The snow crunched beneath his boots as he went to her.

"I can't believe you used lights," she beamed, planting a quick, passionate kiss on him. Craning her neck, she took in the spectacle of the tree. "It's amazing. I think Mrs.

Pendleton would be very happy, despite that a *Carrigan* was doing it."

"I hope so."

"Are we still going to your mom's tonight?" she asked.

"Yes." The moment of truth had arrived. He retrieved the velvet case. "But first, I have something I want to ask you."

As he went down on one knee, her face froze in shock.

Looking up at her, he opened the box, revealing what he'd spent the last six weeks searching for—a round center stone with a twisted vine of smaller gems, all set in a yellow gold band. The design was elegant and sophisticated, just like Skye, while also giving a nod to the natural world that she now inhabited daily with him. "Skylar, will you marry me?"

Her gaze darted from the diamond, to his face, and then back to the diamond. Tears sprang into her eyes. "Yes," she said, her voice thick. "Oh, Joe. Yes."

He removed the ring and slid it onto her left hand, then stood and kissed her carefully, softly, as if they weren't standing outside with cars passing by every few minutes, slowing down to look at the couple embracing on Christmas Eve before a giant and colorfully-lit pine tree.

He cupped her face with his hands. "I love you, Skye."

"I love you too, Carrigan." Then between his kisses, she added, "But tell me one thing—who will own The Peppermint Tree?"

"I thought that was obvious."

He grinned and added, "Our children."

Epilogue

hristmas Eve
Six years later

"I THINK the tree is magical, Daddy."

Joe glanced at his oldest daughter, Sophia. At five years old, she was a mini-Skylar, with russet-colored hair and blue eyes that stole his heart every time he gazed into them. She sat atop her horse with a straight back and confident composure, bundled into a fleece-lined jacket and gloves and very proud to be riding alone for the first time. Sophie had needed something special to fill her day, with Skye back at home caring for the newest addition to the family—three-week-old Lily.

Skye would argue with him later that Sophie wasn't ready to fly solo, but he'd kept a very close eye on his baby girl, and he'd put her on the gentlest and most docile gelding they owned—Skye's own horse, Sarge. And while Sophie had begged him to wear her cowboy hat, he'd been firm that she instead don a rock-climbing helmet made especially for children.

"I think you're right, Peanut," he said.

"How does it get decorated?" She leaned her head back to admire the glittering lights. "Does Santa come early and do it?"

"Something like that." Joe smiled, not wanting to ruin the conclusion she had reached.

Truthfully, decorating The Peppermint Tree was a helluva lot of work that required a crane and about thirty boxes of lights. But knowing how much the women in his life enjoyed it always compelled him to complete the task as soon as Thanksgiving was over.

"Do you think I'll meet my husband here?"

Joe choked on his response, then covered his tracks by pretending to clear his throat. He couldn't imagine handing Sophie off to some random wet-behind-the-ears cowboy with a hankering for his daughter, especially one that she met by a tree. He was a bald-faced hypocrite to be sure, because he'd met Skylar here when they were kids, and she must have shared the story with Sophie. And, of course, his own mother and father had had their first encounter at this very same tree.

"I suppose anything is possible," he conceded.

"Daddy, I don't think Lily should be allowed outside until she's much older." Sophie's voice held an air of authority.

"And why's that?"

"Because she can't walk."

He moved his horse closer to Sarge. "What if Mommy and I carry her for a while?"

She arched an eyebrow. "That seems like a lot of work. Is it really worth it?"

"I think it is, sweetheart. How will Lily visit her grand-mothers if she can never leave the house?"

"Well, they could come to her. Or I could take a photo of her to Gramma's or Nana's house when I go to visit."

"It's a sound argument. I'll talk to Mommy, okay?"

"I'm going to be a lawyer one day," Sophie announced.

"You are?"

She nodded. "I'm going to be just like Mommy."

Joe chuckled. She already was. "I have no doubt of that. We should get back. It's getting cold. And besides, aren't you supposed to make cookies for Santa?"

Sophie grinned and nodded. "Nana's coming to help."

Skye's mother would arrive soon to make goodies with Sophie and help Skye with Christmas Eve dinner. Skye's dad and Joe's mom, along with his brother-in-law, Ollie, his wife, Celeste, and their young daughter would stop by later for a small holiday gathering. Lily had been colicky and not sleeping well, and Skye was exhausted, so Joe had told everyone that they'd need to be gone by eight p.m.

SKYE ROSE from the rocking chair and carried a sleeping Lily to the crib. Very carefully, she placed her precious bundle onto the mattress, not daring to even breathe. Then, with her bare feet making no sound on the wooden floor, she moved backward like a thief in the night to exit the nursery before her beloved second child noticed and came awake like a piglet on steroids.

Only when she was in the hallway, with the door nearly closed—she wouldn't completely shut it since the sound would likely set off her slumbering little munchkin—did her shoulders sag and she inhale precious air. She glanced down and noticed that her left breast was exposed, having nursed Lily to sleep after the Christmas Eve festivities with her family and Joe's mom.

She was about to tuck the milk station back into the unattractive but very practical nursing bra when she turned and bumped into Joe.

"Is this my Christmas present?" he whispered, grinning.

She snickered quietly and pushed his hand away, glancing around his shoulder to make sure Sophie wasn't standing in the hallway watching.

"She's in bed," Joe said, his breath hot against her ear as his large palm covered her exposed nipple.

They hadn't had much alone time the past few weeks. Skye had spent most nights rocking and walking baby Lily, and by the time she and Joe passed each other in the bathroom or the kitchen, Skye's energy level equaled that of a bear seeking immediate hibernation.

She angled her face to his and kissed him hard. "I don't know how much time we'll have," she whispered.

He crushed her against him, lifted her slightly, and with his arms wrapped around her, carried her to their bedroom. When he kicked the door to shut it, she shot from his embrace to stop it from slamming, then carefully closed and locked it.

"You're so reckless," she said quietly, trying to catch her breath.

He started undressing. "Isn't that why you love me?"

"It's one of many reasons." She went to the bed and threw back the covers, her intention to be under them before getting naked.

"Are you cold?" he asked, joining her in all his muscled and nude glory.

"No, I'm just … feeling a little pudgy." She pulled the covers over her stretchy pants and button-down Henley, which was perfect for releasing one of her milk jugs when Lily's stomach rumbled—which occurred about every two hours—but did little to make her enticing to her husband.

Joe sidled close to her, his hand sliding beneath the covers and under her shirt. "Skylar," he said, nuzzling her neck as his fingers kneaded her hips, "I think you're beautiful. And I want you more today than I did in the men's locker room that night." He paused, bracing himself with an elbow so that he could look into her face. "That's saying something, because I'd never wanted anyone as much as I wanted you then."

She released a husky laugh.

"You gave me Sophie, and now Lily, and along with you, those are the most precious gifts in my life." He kissed the tip of her nose. "Please don't ever wonder if I want you. I want you pretty much every second of every day."

Skye swallowed against the tightness in her throat. Joe didn't wear his emotions on his sleeve—in this way, he was very much like his late father—and his words lit a fire in some cold corner of her heart that she hadn't realized had gone neglected.

"Thank you," she said, her hands coming to his face as tears streamed down the sides of her cheeks.

With a burning hunger, she kissed him, her body desperate for his. He made fast work of her clothes, forgoing any foreplay. He joined with her, his muscles clenching with each thrust. She met him equally, clawing at his back, taking as much as giving, selfish in her need not to be left behind.

Her orgasm slammed into her, the pleasure sustaining itself with a pulsing intensity. For an instant, she ceased to be mother, housekeeper, cook, and was simply a woman—wild and desirable.

She always felt this with Carrigan. Only him.

As they recovered amongst tangled sheets, Joe's body still half-covering hers, her mind homed in on one thought.

"You still owe me a pizza," she said, trying to catch her breath.

He lifted his head, his black hair mussed.

"Oh my God, you're right." He grinned. "I never fed you that night. What have we got in the fridge?"

"Well, you're in luck. There's a frozen pizza in the freezer."

"Then I'm on it." He leaned forward and kissed her again, then rose from the bed.

She enjoyed watching his shadowy figure pull on sweat-pants and a t-shirt.

"One pizza coming up, Mrs. Carrigan," he said, leaning down to kiss her one more time. "Anything else?"

She made a sound of content, then shook her head. "This is turning into a near perfect Christmas Eve."

"Then what would make it absolutely perfect?"

"A four-hour block of sleep," she whispered against his mouth.

"I would offer to take care of Lily, but I fear my breasts just won't do."

She sighed. "They won't."

"You could transition her to bottle-feeding," he suggested.

"I know. I will, just not yet." As tired as she was, she liked the closeness of nursing. She wasn't about to give it up anytime soon.

"Come downstairs, and I'll make you some herbal tea to go with your pizza." He glanced down the length of her naked body. "Or, I could just ravage you again."

She chuckled and let him pull her to a standing position.

He pulled her into his arms. "Maybe I'll just ravage you again," he said.

She squirmed out of his arms to find her robe. "Feed me first, ravage me second."

A resounding knock on the bedroom door interrupted them. "Mommy?"

Skye quickly donned the robe and cinched the belt tight as Joe opened the door.

"What is it, sweetie?" Skye asked.

Sophie bounded in the room carrying a piece of paper and handed it to Skye. "I almost forgot about this," she said. "I want to leave it for Santa Claus."

Joe switched on the overhead light as Skye sat on the edge of the bed and pulled Sophie beside her.

Upon the paper, Sophie had drawn a large pine tree with Christmas decorations adorning it. Beside it was a woman and written in Sophie's large block letters—a few of them backward—was THANK YOU FOR THE SKY.

"What is this?" Skye asked.

"When Daddy took me to The Peppermint Tree today, I saw her."

Skye frowned. "Saw who?"

Sophie pointed at the lady in the drawing. "Her."

Skye glanced up at Joe, who stood beside them. He gave a shake of his head. He hadn't seen any woman.

"She said, 'Thank you for the sky,'" Sophie said, then wrinkled her forehead. "Or maybe it was 'Thank you to the sky.'"

"Did the woman tell you her name?" Joe asked.

Sophie went silent, her expression conveying her think-ing-mode. "Charlotte." She smiled, obviously thrilled with her recall.

A chill went down Skye's spine. "Charlotte Pendleton?"

"How do you know her last name?" Sophie asked.

"Lucky guess," Skye replied.

She caught Joe's eye again, who watched her with amuse-ment shining in his gaze.

"I think maybe Mrs. Pendleton was thanking us for taking care of The Peppermint Tree," Skye told her daughter. "And it's really nice that you drew this picture. Now, I think you need to get back in bed, so Santa can visit us tonight. I'll be sure and put your drawing downstairs by the milk and cookies."

"Okay," Sophie said.

Skye took her daughter's hand, and she and Joe led Sophie back to her bed and tucked her in. Then, they headed downstairs for pizza and tea. A fire glowed softly in the hearth.

Skye placed the drawing near the Christmas tree, and thought of the other tree—The Peppermint Tree—just beyond in the woods.

Joe came up behind her, encircling her in his arms.

"How do you explain that?" he asked.

"I don't know," Skye admitted. "But I think Mrs. Pendleton is happy with what we've done with the place, and the tree. I'm glad you found me that night on the highway."

"We were meant to be together." He nuzzled the side of her cheek. "It just took us a while to come around to it. Sophie asked me if she would meet her husband by The Peppermint Tree one day."

Skye grinned up at him. "I can imagine your response, but I told you, the tree is magic."

He groaned. "Well, then there's only one thing to do."

"What's that?"

"I'm building a ten-foot wall around the damned thing."

Laughing, she spun around, locking her arms around his neck.

"It won't matter," she said. "Fate will always find a way." Then she kissed him.

THE END

. . .

IF YOU ENJOYED *The Peppermint Tree*, would you consider posting a review? Not only does this help other readers discover a story, but it also aids an author in pursuing promotional opportunities. My sincere gratitude. ~ Kristy

About the Author

Kristy McCaffrey has been writing since she was very young, but it wasn't until she was a stay-at-home mom that she considered becoming published. A fascination with science led her to earn two mechanical engineering degrees—she did her undergraduate work at Arizona State University and her graduate studies at the University of Pittsburgh—but story-telling has always been her passion. She writes both contemporary tales and award-winning historical western romances.

An Arizona native, Kristy and her husband reside in the desert where they frequently remove (rescue) rattlesnakes from their property, go for runs among the cactus, and plan trips to far-off places like the Orkney Islands or Machu Picchu. But mostly, she works 12-hour days and enjoys at-home date nights with her sweetheart, which usually include Will Ferrell movies and sci-fi flicks. Her four children have nearly all flown the nest, and the family recently lost their cherished chocolate Labrador, Ranger, so these days a great deal of attention is lavished on Ranger's sister, Lily, and the newest addition to the household—Marley, an older yellow Labrador they rescued in early 2018. Both dogs are frequently featured on Kristy's Instagram account, so pop over to meet her canine family.

To stay updated on Kristy's newest releases, be sure to sign up for her newsletter, visit her website, or follow her at BookBub.

Connect with Kristy

Website: kmccaffrey.com
Newsletter: kmccaffrey.com/subscribe/
Facebook: facebook.com/AuthorKristyMcCaffrey
Twitter: twitter.com/McCaffreyKristy
Instagram: instagram.com/kristymccaffrey/
BookBub: bookbub.com/authors/kristy-mccaffrey

Don't miss Kristy's Award-Winning Wings of the West Series

Historical Western Romances

Experience the grit, the hope, and the romance of the Old West.

Learn more at Kristy's website
https://kmccaffrey.com/

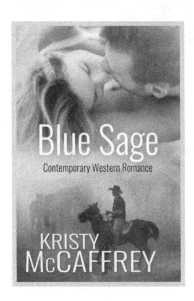

Blue Sage
Contemporary Western Romance

KRISTY McCAFFREY

What do you do when a woman literally lands at your feet?

Braden Delaney has taken over the family cattle business after the death of his father, but faced with difficult financial decisions, he contemplates selling a portion of the massive Delaney ranch holdings known as Whisper Rock, a place of unusual occurrences. The sudden appearance of a pretty relic-hunter while he's collecting his livestock, however, is about to change his mind.

Archaeologist Audrey Driggs arrives in the remote wilderness of Northern Arizona for clues to a life-altering experience from her childhood. When she rolls off a mountain and lands at the feet of rugged cowboy Braden Delaney, it's clear she needs his knowledge of the area to complete her quest. But if she tells him the truth, will he think she's crazy?

Together, they'll uncover a long-lost secret.

Learn more at
https://kmccaffrey.com/blue-sage/

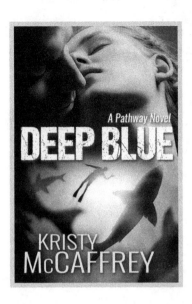

Don't miss this first book in a sexy and suspenseful new series!!

In the deep blue ocean lives an ancient predator...

Dr. Grace Mann knows great white sharks. As the daughter of an obsessed shark researcher based at the Farallon Islands, Grace spent her childhood in the company of these elegant and massive creatures. When a photo of her freediving with a great white goes viral, the institute where she works seeks to capitalize on her new-found fame by producing a documentary about her work.

Underwater filmmaker Alec Galloway admires Dr. Mann and jumps at the opportunity to create a film showcasing the pretty biologist. As he heads to Guadalupe Island in Baja California Sur for a three-week expedition, it's clear that his fan-boy crush on Grace is turning into something more serious. But even more pressing—Grace's passionate focus on the sharks just might get her killed.

Learn more at
https://kmccaffrey.com/deep-blue/

CPSIA information can be obtained
at www.ICGtesting.com
Printed in the USA
LVHW082307190921
698227LV00023B/620